Writing the Critical Essay

Gays in the Military

An **OPPOSING** **VIEWPOINTS®** Guide

Lauri S. Friedman, *Book Editor*

GREENHAVEN PRESS
A part of Gale, Cengage Learning

GALE
CENGAGE Learning

Detroit • New York • San Francisco • New Haven, Conn • Waterville, Maine • London

Elizabeth Des Chenes, *Managing Editor*

© 2012 Greenhaven Press, a part of Gale, Cengage Learning

Gale and Greenhaven Press are registered trademarks used herein under license.

For more information, contact:
Greenhaven Press
27500 Drake Rd.
Farmington Hills, MI 48331-3535
Or you can visit our Internet site at gale.cengage.com

ALL RIGHTS RESERVED.
No part of this work covered by the copyright herein may be reproduced, transmitted, stored, or used in any form or by any means graphic, electronic, or mechanical, including but not limited to photocopying, recording, scanning, digitizing, taping, Web distribution, information networks, or information storage and retrieval systems, except as permitted under Section 107 or 108 of the 1976 United States Copyright Act, without the prior written permission of the publisher.

For product information and technology assistance, contact us at

Gale Customer Support, 1-800-877-4253
For permission to use material from this text or product, submit all requests online at www.cengage.com/permissions

Further permissions questions can be e-mailed to permissionrequest@cengage.com

Articles in Greenhaven Press anthologies are often edited for length to meet page requirements. In addition, original titles of these works are changed to clearly present the main thesis and to explicitly indicate the author's opinion. Every effort is made to ensure that Greenhaven Press accurately reflects the original intent of the authors. Every effort has been made to trace the owners of copyrighted material.

Cover image © Brooks Kraft/Corbis.

LIBRARY OF CONGRESS CATALOGING-IN-PUBLICATION DATA

Gays in the military / Lauri S. Friedman, book editor.
  p. cm. -- (Writing the critical essay: an opposing viewpoints guide)
  Includes bibliographical references and index.
  ISBN 978-0-7377-5912-9 (hardcover)
  1. Gay military personnel--United States. I. Friedman, Lauri S.
  UB418.G38G3728 2012
  355.0086'640973--dc23
                                                                    2011032689

Printed in the United States of America
1 2 3 4 5 6 7 15 14 13 12 11

CONTENTS

YA
355.0086
GAY

Foreword   5

Introduction   7
   Beyond "Don't Ask, Don't Tell"

Section One: Opposing Viewpoints on Gays in the Military

Viewpoint One: Gay Soldiers Should Be Allowed to Serve Openly   13
   Gabriel Arana

Viewpoint Two: Gay Soldiers Should Not Be Allowed to Serve Openly   21
   Stuart Koehl

Viewpoint Three: Allowing Gay Soldiers to Serve Openly Protects Them from Harm   29
   Joseph Rocha

Viewpoint Four: Allowing Gay Soldiers to Serve Openly Puts Them at Risk   39
   Eric Harbin

Viewpoint Five: Allowing Gays to Serve Openly Will Strengthen the US Military   45
   Stephen Benjamin

Viewpoint Six: Allowing Gays to Serve Openly Will Weaken the US Military   52
   Robert G. Marshall

Section Two: Model Essays and Writing Exercises

Preface A: The Five-Paragraph Essay   59

Preface B: The Persuasive Essay   61

Essay One: America's Confusion: Openly Gay
Soldiers and Civil Rights in the Military   64

   Exercise 1A: Create an Outline from an
       Existing Essay   68

   Exercise 1B: Create an Outline for Your
       Own Essay   69

Essay Two: A Gay-Friendly Military Is a
Weakened Military   72

   Exercise 2A: Create an Outline from an
       Existing Essay   75

   Exercise 2B: Identify Persuasive Techniques   75

Essay Three: The Military's Loss   77

   Exercise 3A: Examining Introductions and
       Conclusions   83

   Exercise 3B: Using Quotations to Enliven
       Your Essay   84

Final Writing Challenge: Write Your Own
Persuasive Five-Paragraph Essay   86

Section Three: Supporting Research Material

Appendix A: Facts About Gays in the Military   90

Appendix B: Finding and Using Sources
of Information   98

Appendix C: Using MLA Style to Create a Works
Cited List   101

Appendix D: Sample Essay Topics on Gays
in the Military   104

Organizations to Contact   106

Bibliography   110

Index   116

Picture Credits   119

About the Editor   120

Foreword

Examining the state of writing and how it is taught in the United States was the official purpose of the National Commission on Writing in America's Schools and Colleges. The commission, made up of teachers, school administrators, business leaders, and college and university presidents, released its first report in 2003. "Despite the best efforts of many educators," commissioners argued, "writing has not received the full attention it deserves." Among the findings of the commission was that most fourth-grade students spent less than three hours a week writing, that three-quarters of high school seniors never receive a writing assignment in their history or social studies classes, and that more than 50 percent of first-year students in college have problems writing error-free papers. The commission called for a "cultural sea change" that would increase the emphasis on writing for both elementary and secondary schools. These conclusions have made some educators realize that writing must be emphasized in the curriculum. As colleges are demanding an ever-higher level of writing proficiency from incoming students, schools must respond by making students more competent writers. In response to these concerns, the SAT, an influential standardized test used for college admissions, required an essay for the first time in 2005.

Books in the Writing the Critical Essay: An Opposing Viewpoints Guide series use the patented Opposing Viewpoints format to help students learn to organize ideas and arguments and to write essays using common critical writing techniques. Each book in the series focuses on a particular type of essay writing—including expository, persuasive, descriptive, and narrative—that students learn while being taught both the five-paragraph essay as well as longer pieces of writing that have an opinionated focus. These guides include everything necessary to help students research, outline, draft, edit, and ultimately write successful essays across the curriculum, including essays for the SAT.

Using Opposing Viewpoints

This series is inspired by and builds upon Greenhaven Press's acclaimed Opposing Viewpoints series. As in the parent series, each book in the Writing the Critical Essay series focuses on a timely and controversial social issue that provides lots of opportunities for creating thought-provoking essays. The first section of each volume begins with a brief introductory essay that provides context for the opposing viewpoints that follow. These articles are chosen for their accessibility and clearly stated views. The thesis of each article is made explicit in the article's title and is accentuated by its pairing with an opposing or alternative view. These essays are both models of persuasive writing techniques and valuable research material that students can mine to write their own informed essays. Guided reading and discussion questions help lead students to key ideas and writing techniques presented in the selections.

The second section of each book begins with a preface discussing the format of the essays and examining characteristics of the featured essay type. Model five-paragraph and longer essays then demonstrate that essay type. The essays are annotated so that key writing elements and techniques are pointed out to the student. Sequential, step-by-step exercises help students construct and refine thesis statements; organize material into outlines; analyze and try out writing techniques; write transitions, introductions, and conclusions; and incorporate quotations and other researched material. Ultimately, students construct their own compositions using the designated essay type.

The third section of each volume provides additional research material and writing prompts to help the student. Additional facts about the topic of the book serve as a convenient source of supporting material for essays. Other features help students go beyond the book for their research. Like other Greenhaven Press books, each book in the Writing the Critical Essay series includes bibliographic listings of relevant periodical articles, books, websites, and organizations to contact.

Writing the Critical Essay: An Opposing Viewpoints Guide will help students master essay techniques that can be used in any discipline.

Introduction

Beyond "Don't Ask, Don't Tell"

At the heart of contemporary debates over gays in the military is the policy known as "Don't Ask, Don't Tell," or DADT. This policy was signed into law by President Bill Clinton in the early 1990s, at a time when gay people were banned from serving in the military. DADT changed that, but only slightly: Under DADT, only *openly* gay soldiers were banned. In other words, gay soldiers were permitted to serve, as long as no one knew they were gay. To achieve this balance, DADT prohibited military applicants from being asked about their sexual orientation (the "Don't Ask" part of the policy). In return, soldiers were not allowed to disclose their sexuality, lest they be penalized with discharge (the "Don't Tell" part of the policy.) DADT was intended to be a compromise between those who wanted gay people to be allowed to serve and those who did not.

It is sometimes said that a compromise is when neither party gets what they want, and this is probably true of DADT. The policy left much to be desired among those who both opposed and supported it. For supporters of gay rights, the policy did not go far enough: They claimed it perpetuated the discrimination of gay soldiers and forced them to lie about who they are even as they put their lives on the line for their country. For opponents of DADT, the policy challenged the long-standing belief that homosexuality is incompatible with military service because of the threat it poses to unit cohesion, military readiness, and behavioral standards.

For the next seventeen years, the military and the country adjusted to the change in policy. It is likely that many gay soldiers served honorably yet quietly. A comprehensive survey undertaken by the Department of Defense in 2010 found that nearly 70 percent of service members believe they have probably served with someone who is gay. More precise is the number of gay soldiers who served less quietly: By 2011, more than fourteen thousand service members had been discharged because they either confessed to being homosexual or were outed by a third party.

As the twenty-first century progressed, several realities put stress on both the DADT policy and the military in general. The United States found itself deeply committed to wars in both Iraq and Afghanistan, which in 2010 surpassed the Vietnam War in becoming the longest conflict in US history. These conflicts, combined with the ongoing War on Terror, forced enlisted men and women to do multiple tours of duty and left recruiters scrambling to find enough qualified applicants to meet enlistment quotas. At the same time that the all-volunteer military force found itself stretched thin, the early twenty-first century witnessed a surge of interest in pursuing gay rights in other sectors of society, as demonstrated by several states' decisions to legalize same-sex marriage.

It was in this environment that President Barack Obama sought to repeal DADT on the grounds that it unfairly discriminated against some of America's bravest citizens at a time when the country could least afford to do so. "We should not be punishing patriotic Americans who have stepped forward to serve the country," he said in 2009. "We should be celebrating their willingness to step forward and show such courage . . . especially when we are fighting two wars."[1] Support grew for repeal in 2010 after several key figures came out in support of the change, including secretary of defense Robert Gates and US Navy admiral Mike Mullen, chairman of the Joint Chiefs of Staff. "Allowing gays and lesbians to serve openly would be the right thing to do," Mullen testified in February 2010. "No matter how I look at this issue, I cannot escape being troubled by the fact that we have in place a policy which forces young men and women to lie about who they are in order to defend their fellow citizens."[2] Mullen expressed confidence that the military would be able to adapt to such a change, and his was an influential and credible voice on the matter. Another key moment for repeal occurred in September 2010, when US district judge Virginia Phillips ruled that DADT was unconstitutional, a violation of the First and Fifth Amendment rights of gay Americans.

After much political back-and-forth, repeal of the policy eventually passed in both the House and Senate and was signed into law by Obama on December 22, 2010. "We are not a nation that says, 'don't ask, don't tell,'" he declared, as he authorized the Don't Ask, Don't Tell Repeal Act of 2010. "We are a nation that says, 'Out of many, we are one.' We are a nation that welcomes the service of every patriot. We are a nation that believes that all men and women are created equal. Those are the ideals that generations have fought for. Those are the ideals that we uphold today."[3]

The repeal did not become law right away, however. After repeal of the DADT policy was approved by Congress and signed by the president, it went through a certification process. This process required the president, the secretary of defense, and the chairman of the Joint Chiefs of Staff to all agree that repealing the DADT policy would not harm military readiness, military effectiveness, unit cohesion, and recruitment and retention. The repeal was eventually certified on July 22, 2011, and went through a final sixty-day waiting period before becoming law on September 20, 2011. Even after these milestones were reached, however, the military was still faced with the issue of implementing procedures to account for the new reality of openly gay soldiers among the ranks. Former marine Mackubin Thomas Owens of the Foreign Policy Research Institute posed just some of the many questions that still needed to be addressed as the military designed the post-DADT era:

> Are there any assignments to which homosexuals must be or may not be assigned? . . . Will homosexuals be promoted at a faster rate to "compensate"

for previous years of discrimination? What benefits will same-sex "partners" receive? How long must one have a relationship to qualify as a partner? Will partners of homosexuals be assigned to on-base housing? Do former partners of active duty homosexuals retain dependent benefits (like a divorced spouse) when divorce is not a legal option? Will homosexual service members be permitted to date each other? Live with each other as partners in bachelor officer quarters (BOQ) or bachelor enlisted quarters (BEQ)? How does this affect fraternization regulations? Will homosexuals be deployed to countries where homosexuality is a crime? If not, who picks up the slack?[4]

How the military will absorb openly gay soldiers into its ranks is just one of the issues surrounding the repeal of Don't Ask, Don't Tell and just one of the topics explored in *Writing the Critical Essay: Gays in the Military*. Cogently argued viewpoints and model essays explore how openly gay soldiers might affect military readiness and unit cohesion and whether allowing openly gay soldiers to fight puts them in harm's way or protects them from harm. The place of homosexuality in the military is also considered, as is the issue of how the presence of openly gay soldiers affects the quality of the all-volunteer force. Thought-provoking writing exercises and step-by-step instructions help readers write their own five-paragraph persuasive essays on this complicated and timely subject.

Notes

1. Quoted in Associated Press, "Obama: I'll Let Gays Serve Openly in Military," MSNBC.com, October 10, 2009. www.msnbc.msn.com/id/33255971/ns/politics-white_house/t/obama-ill-let-gays-serve-openly-military/.

2. "Testimony Regarding DoD 'Don't Ask, Don't Tell' Policy," Washington, DC, February 2, 2010. www.jcs.mil/speech.aspx?id = 1322.
3. Remarks by the President and Vice President at Signing of the Don't Ask, Don't Tell Repeal Act of 2010, December 22, 2010. www.whitehouse.gov/the-press-office/2010/12/22/remarks-president-and-vice-president-signing-dont-ask-dont-tell-repeal-a.
4. Mackubin Thomas Owens, "Repealing 'Don't Ask' Will Weaken the US Military," *Weekly Standard*, December 3, 2010. www.weeklystandard.com/blogs/repealing-dont-ask-will-weaken-us-military_520652.html?nopager = 1.

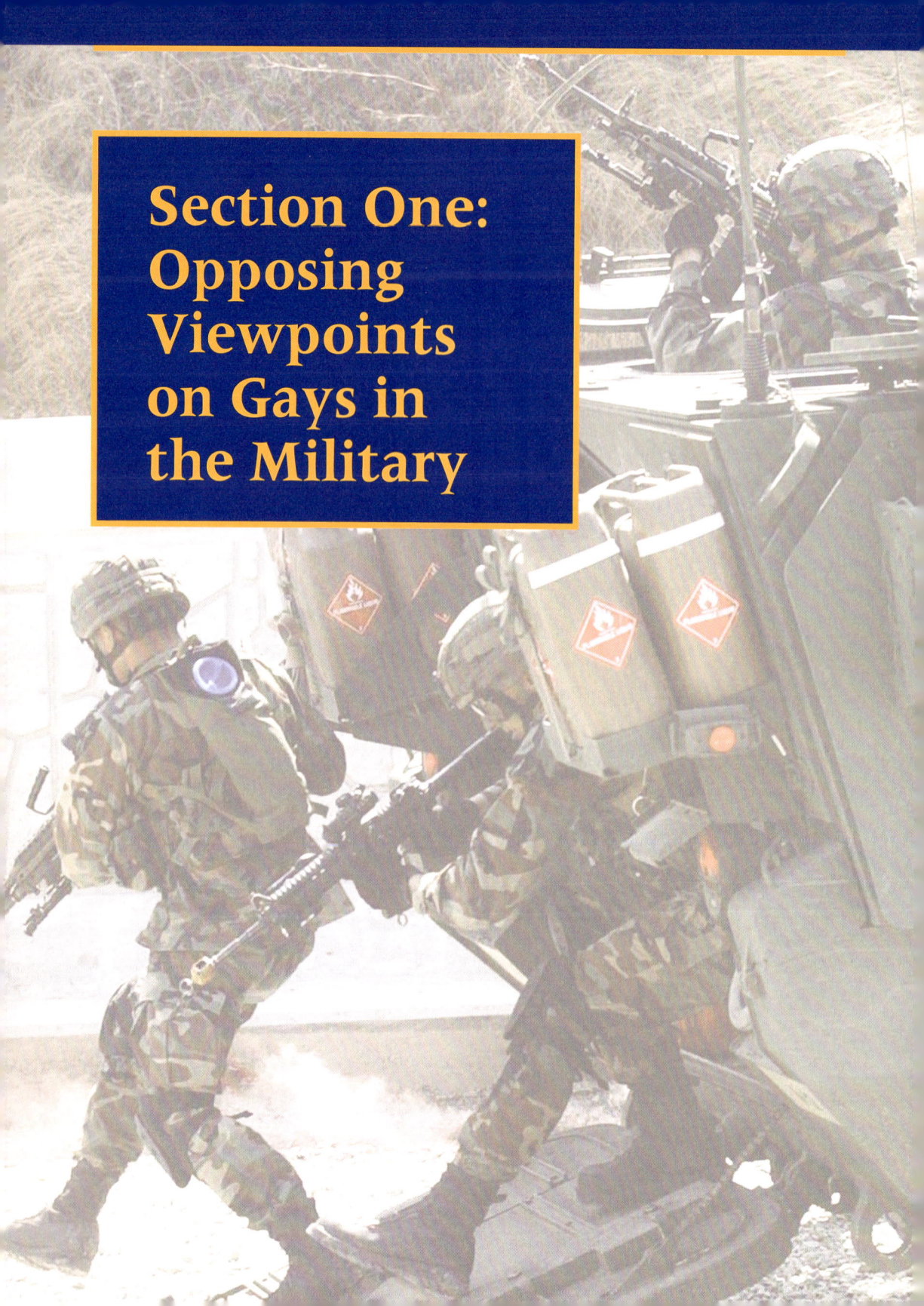
Section One: Opposing Viewpoints on Gays in the Military

Gay Soldiers Should Be Allowed to Serve Openly

Viewpoint One

Gabriel Arana

In the following essay Gabriel Arana argues that gay soldiers should be free to serve openly. He says that since the adoption of Don't Ask, Don't Tell (DADT) in 1993, gay and lesbian soldiers had been harassed, intimidated, and physically assaulted because no law existed to protect them. Thousands had been dismissed for admitting their sexuality. Arana argues that this is unjust and un-American—military soldiers should not be forced to lie and hide who they are. By not letting gay soldiers serve openly, Arana asserts that Americans gave tacit approval to homophobia and discrimination. He concludes that DADT institutionalized prejudice, bigotry, and deception while letting gay soldiers serve openly promotes freedom, tolerance, and justice.

Arana is web editor at the *American Prospect,* a liberal political magazine. His work has also appeared in the *Nation, Slate,* the *Advocate,* and the *Daily Beast.*

Consider the following questions:
1. How many soldiers does Arana say have been let go under DADT since 1993?
2. What effect does Arana say DADT had on straight female soldiers?
3. Who is Barry Winchell and how does he factor into the author's argument?

Joseph Rocha spent years as an enlisted soldier working to move his way up. He wanted to enroll in the U.S. Naval Academy to be an officer in the United States Marine Corps. He volunteered for difficult assignments

Gabriel Arana, "Bigotry Boot Camp," *American Prospect,* September 16, 2010. www.prospect.org. All rights reserved. Reproduced by permission.

US marine Joseph Rocha endured years of relentless physical and psychological taunting in the service. When he finally told his superiors he was gay, he was discharged.

and earned certifications in martial arts, combat, and swimming—all the while his fellow soldiers harassed him about his sexual orientation. They pressured him to sleep with prostitutes and, when he would not, asked him if he was a "faggot." His commanding officer openly referred to him as gay and looked the other way as Rocha was made to simulate oral sex on men and beaten on his 19th birthday. After years of relentless taunting, he finally cracked, told his superiors he was gay, and was quickly discharged.

Rocha is just one of the 13,500 armed forces personnel who have been let go under "don't ask, don't tell" (DADT) since the law was signed by President Bill Clinton in 1993. His was one of the many unsettling stories that a federal judge in California highlighted in ruling the policy unconstitutional last week. But the decision may not have to wind its way through the appellate courts before gay service members get their due. Next week, the Senate plans to take up the annual Defense Authorization Bill, which includes an amendment to repeal DADT. The House has already approved a similar bill, and President Barack Obama—who since taking office has weathered substantial criticism from the gay-rights community for stalling on repeal—has promised to sign it.

Alexander Nicholson of the Servicemembers Legal Defense Network, a gay-rights group that has long opposed DADT, has said he is "fairly confident" the measure to repeal it has the requisite 60 votes to pass. If it does, it will bring a belated end to nearly 20 years of systematic discrimination in one of our most vaunted institutions. But as the legacy of a more intolerant era, "don't ask, don't tell" also serves as a historical lesson in how social institutions enshrine—and more important, perpetuate—bigotry.

"When your chain of command, your institution is making a clear statement that gay, lesbian, and bisexual people are essentially second-class, it filters down to create an environment in which people feel empowered to have negative attitudes toward gay, lesbian, and bisexual people—and act in ways that reflect them," says Melissa Sheridan Embser-Herbert, a professor of sociology at Hamline University who studies the social dynamics in the military. She is also a former member of the U.S. Army and Army Reserve.

DADT supporters like John McCain pledge to "support the men and women of the military" and "fight what is clearly a political agenda" by filibustering the repeal, but the ban on openly gay service members has never been about the troops. From the start, it was a top-down

> ## Allowing Openly Gay Soldiers to Serve Protects Their Civil Rights
>
> [DADT] was an inane policy that had the military brass sticking its collective head in the sand while gays and lesbians honorably served to defend the very liberties they were being denied. The federal government legally discriminates against homosexual military personnel while protecting federal civilian employees from the same injustice. The U.S. Office of Personnel Management website states, "As the nation's largest employer, the federal government sets an example for other employers that employment discrimination based upon sexual orientation is not acceptable."
>
> Paul James, "Let Open Bias Follow 'Don't Ask, Don't Tell' into Dustbin of History," *Palm Beach (FL) Post*, December 22, 2010. http://www.palmbeachpost.com/opinion/commentary/commentary-let-open-bias-follow-dont-ask-dont-1140709.html.

decision imposed by the Joint Chiefs of Staff and other high-ranking military officials.

At the direction of President Clinton, in 1993 then–Secretary of Defense Les Aspin commissioned the RAND Corporation to study the possible effects of allowing openly gay military members. RAND brought together 75 social scientists who produced an exhaustive 500-page study. They concluded: Though lifting the outright ban on gay service members—which was then the policy but not the law—would require a period of adjustment to allow training officers on the new policy, openly gay military service posed no threat to "unit cohesion," morale, or "military readiness." After spending $1.3 million for the study, the Pentagon did everything possible to keep

Americans Think Gay Men and Women Should Be Allowed to Serve Openly

A 2010 poll taken by CNN found the majority of Americans favored letting gay men and women serve openly in the military.

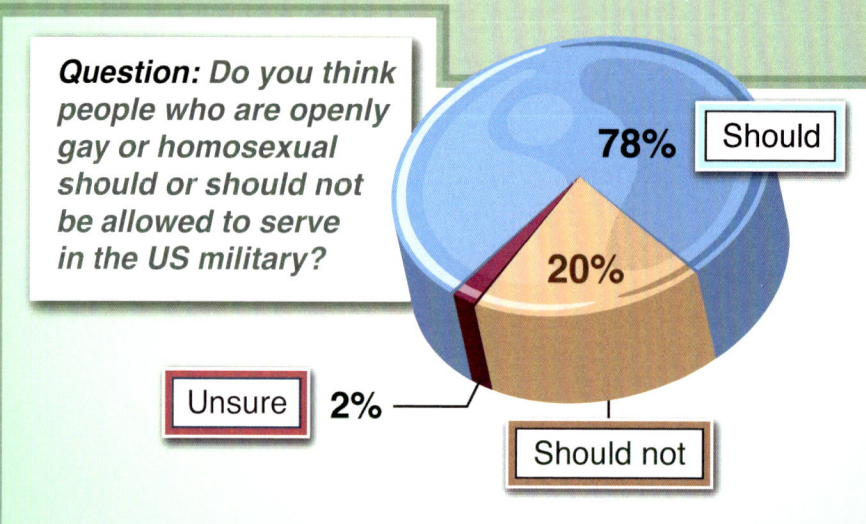

Question: Do you think people who are openly gay or homosexual should or should not be allowed to serve in the US military?

- Should 78%
- Should not 20%
- Unsure 2%

Taken from: Quinnipiac University Poll, February 2–8, 2010.

it from going public; according to *The New York Times*, it didn't even bother consulting the report.

Instead, the Department of Defense relied on a flimsy 15-page "review" by five senior generals and admirals that determined—without bothering to cite any evidence—that "all homosexuality is incompatible with military service" and that allowing gays in the military would lead to the spread of diseases like AIDS. The Joint Chiefs used this to push back on President Clinton, who ultimately gave in and settled for "don't ask, don't tell," which allowed gay men and women to serve as long as no one knew about their sexual orientation.

At the time, DADT was touted as a "compromise" between an all-out ban and an open-door policy—not the desired outcome but at least a step forward. But in reality, it made things worse. The number of soldiers given the boot on account of their sexual orientation surged after the policy was implemented. Previously, each branch had its own policy for dealing with gays in the ranks, allowing at least some latitude in deciding whether to dismiss a gay service member. Now military officers were required by federal law to root out gays. And as *Slate*'s Brian Palmer has reported, "don't ask, don't tell" was perhaps a misnomer; there was a steep penalty for telling but a strong incentive for asking. According to the Servicemembers Legal Defense Network, the policy led to gay witch hunts.

Harassment—both verbal and physical—of gay soldiers actually increased, and it's not difficult to understand why. DADT was nothing if not an effort to enforce—and penalize deviations from—masculine norms. And what better way to show you're a real man than by picking on the little guy?

"It has fostered an environment where sexuality is at the center, and it makes people have to do everything they can to make sure they're perceived as heterosexual," Embser-Herbert says. "Regardless of sexual orientation, if a guy isn't as macho as someone else, you now have a government-mandated mechanism for making his life miserable."

DADT turned sexuality into a weapon, and it isn't just gay soldiers who have suffered. For fear of being labeled as lesbians—a real threat given that DADT-related discharges disproportionally involve women—many women have chosen not to report sexual harassment from male colleagues.

In 2000, the Pentagon finally confronted the epidemic of harassment in the armed forces after fellow soldiers brutally beat Barry Winchell, an infantry soldier in the Army, to death with a baseball bat as he slept in his barracks. In the wake of the incident, the Department of Defense conducted a study that found 80 percent of service members had heard their colleagues use gay slurs or tell gay jokes and 85 percent reported the jokes were tolerated by other service members or their superiors. In addition, 37 percent said they had witnessed their colleagues harass a particular service member for his or her perceived sexual orientation.

The policy has also helped anti-gay attitudes persist in the military, even as public sentiment toward gays has warmed. It's true that the military has long been more wary of gays than [has the] broader society. In 1993, more than three-fourths of military members opposed allowing gays in the military, compared with around 60 percent of the public. Some of the disparity between civilian and military attitudes is no doubt because service members are more likely to be Republican and religious, but the chasm between public and military opinion has only widened since DADT took effect. Today, public support for the ban has plummeted to around 20 percent while military members still oppose it by a nearly two-to-three margin.

Just as troubling as the prejudice DADT promotes is the fact that it withholds the antidote. Public attitudes toward gay rights have softened for many reasons, but chief among them is that in 1993, most Americans did

not personally know a gay person, which studies show is the single best predictor of homophobic attitudes. Today, more than 75 percent of Americans have an openly gay co-worker, family member, or friend. In contrast, members of the military have been denied the opportunity to challenge their prejudices and stereotypes about gay people by having openly gay colleagues and superiors whom they respect.

"There is just no education," says Christopher Ness, deputy policy director for the Palm Center, a research institute at the University of California, Santa Barbara, dedicated to studying sexual minorities in the military. "It's an affirmative stigma that prevents an actual dialogue and keeps the services—not just gay troops—in the closet."

In 1993, 60 percent of the American people supported DADT, but by 2011 that support had dropped to 20 percent and there was a corresponding increase in the percentage of people who supported its repeal.

DADT supporters, of course, would like to keep it that way. Tony Perkins, president of the conservative Family Research Council, unwittingly reveals the real danger of letting gays serve openly: In a recent op-ed defending DADT, he warned that repealing the policy would "indoctrinate [military members] into the myths of the homosexual movement: that people are born 'gay' and cannot change and that homosexual conduct does no harm to the individual or to society." As long as the prejudices of people like Perkins are what guide our military personnel policy, DADT will continue to make it a place where only people like him feel comfortable serving.

Analyze the essay:

1. Gabriel Arana quotes from several sources to support the points he makes in his essay. Make a list of all the people he quotes, including their credentials and the nature of their comments. Then pick the quote you found most persuasive. Why did you choose it? What did it lend to Arana's argument?

2. Part of Arana's argument centers around the idea that people in the military are intolerant because they are less likely to know an openly gay person than the rest of the public. Thus, he says, they have been denied opportunities to challenge or correct stereotypes. Think about whether you know any openly gay or lesbian people. Have these people affected the way in which you perceive homosexuals in general? Why or why not?

Gay Soldiers Should Not Be Allowed to Serve Openly

Viewpoint Two

Stuart Koehl

In the following essay Stuart Koehl, a frequent contributor to the conservative *Weekly Standard*, argues that gay soldiers should not be allowed to serve openly. In his opinion, military camaraderie is built on platonic relationships of equal value; introducing sexual tension or prioritized relationships to military units undermines their ability to function as a tight-knit group. He says gay soldiers make other soldiers uncomfortable. They compromise privacy and unit cohesion and disrupt military function, too, in his opinion. Koehl contends that gays do not have the right to serve in the military, because military service is not a right—the military routinely turns people away from service for a number of reasons relating to whether they would make a good soldier. He concludes that historically, armies have refused to let homosexuals serve openly because they compromise an army's ability to function effectively. For all of these reasons, Koehl opposes allowing gays to serve openly in the armed forces.

Consider the following questions:
1. What does the word *agape* mean as used by Koehl?
2. In what way will gay soldiers introduce the problem of favoritism into the military, according to the author?
3. What percentage of the population is homosexual, according to Koehl?

Stuart Koehl, "Don't Repeal 'Don't Ask/Don't Tell,'" *Weekly Standard*, June 15, 2010. www.weeklystandard.com. All rights reserved. Reproduced by permission.

In Stephen Pressfield's novel *Gates of Fire*, the Spartans at Thermopylae, knowing in the morning they will "Dine in Hades," debate among themselves the question, "What is the opposite of fear?" The men give various answers—courage, hatred, anger, duty—but Deinokles, the hero of the piece, has the last word. Looking at his comrades, tired, filthy, bruised, many wounded, he shakes his head and says, "The opposite of fear is love."

The Military Needs Camaraderie, Not Love

This is absolutely true. That which overcomes fear in battle is love—the love of the members of the primary group for each other. But it is a very special sort of love. The Greeks had a word for it: *agape*, the total and selfless love that God has for mankind. Opposed to *agape* stands *eros*, passionate love with overtones of sexual desire and possession.

The military cultivates *agape* in its ranks, but has no room for *eros*. *Agape* will inspire a man to sacrifice his life for a comrade. *Agape* keeps him in his place alongside his friends. Countless observers have seen and written about this. Combat veterans intuitively understand it, even if they have difficulty putting their feelings into words. This particular type of *agape* is unique to men in a purely military setting—because nowhere else are the conditions as extreme and the stakes as high. Whenever sex is introduced, whether hetero or homo, *eros* raises its head and group cohesion crumbles. . . .

As [former secretary of state and chairman of the Joint Chiefs of Staff] Colin Powell once put it, *Men don't like to take showers with men who like to take showers with men*. We're back to the problem of *eros* vs. *agape*.

Homosexuals Undermine Military Discipline

Historically, most armies have seen homosexual behavior as undermining military discipline. Even the Spartans

Former Joint Chiefs of Staff chairman Colin Powell initially opposed DADT, stating that "men don't like to take showers with men who like to take showers with men."

didn't tolerate it in the field, while the Romans considered it a capital offense. There is just one noteworthy example of open homosexuality in military service—the Theban Sacred Band, 150 pairs of homosexual lovers who swore an oath to stand by each other to death (and who were wiped out by Alexander the Great at Cheironeia). So even fairly tolerant societies found homosexuality unacceptable in the army, for the same reason that women were unacceptable: they introduced sexual tension into small-group dynamics, undermining unit cohesion.

Active Duty Troops Do Not Want Gays to Serve Openly

A 2010 poll of active duty troops found the majority either opposed or strongly opposed the overturning of the Don't Ask, Don't Tell policy that prevented gay and lesbian soldiers from openly serving in the military. They said serving with openly gay men and women would make them uncomfortable.

Question: *All in all, do you strongly favor, favor, oppose, or strongly oppose allowing gays and lesbians to serve openly in the military?*

Strongly favor	14.5%
Favor	15%
Neutral	18.7%
Oppose	14.2%
Strongly oppose	36.8%
Decline to answer	0.8%

Question: *If the policy were overturned, how comfortable would you be sharing the following living facilities with an openly gay service member of the same gender?* (Asked only of Army and Marine Corps respondents).

	Comfortable	Uncomfortable	Neutral/Decline to answer
The bunk above or below yours	34.1%	51.8%	14.1%
Barracks room	34.9%	51.5%	13.7%
Barracks building	46.9%	32.3%	20.7%
On-post family housing area	49.9%	28.4%	21.8%
Gym, swimming pool, or recreational facility	48.6%	31.2%	20.3%
Shower	30.3%	57.6%	12.1%
Toilet	38.5%	44.4%	17.1%
Containerized Housing Unit (CHU) or large tent	37.6%	47.2%	15.2%
Small tent or combat outpost	35.6%	49.7%	14.8%

Taken from: Quinnipiac University Poll, February 2–8, 2010.

That tension has several causes. First, heterosexual men in the unit may not like becoming potential objects of sexual attraction to their fellow soldiers (the same thing also applies to women in mixed units), especially given the close quarters and lack of privacy that is part of field service. Second, there may be the suspicion that one or more soldiers may actually have entered into a sexual relationship, with the disruptive effect that can have on both discipline and performance (i.e., favoritism—will this guy risk his life to save me, or will he look out for his "special friend" first). If the homosexual involved is an officer, it creates all sorts of opportunities for abuse, which we have already seen in sexually mixed units. Given the kind of minefield that civilian workplaces have become due to sexual harassment laws, one wonders about the wisdom of tossing metaphorical mines in among the real ones with which our troops have to contend.

> **Military Service Is Not a Civil Right**
>
> People cannot serve in uniform if they are too old or too young, too fat or too thin, too tall or too short, disabled, not sufficiently educated and so on. This, too, might be illegal in the civil sector. So why should exclusion of gay people rise to the status of a civil-rights issue, when denying entry to, say, unmarried individuals with sole custody of dependents under 18, does not?
>
> Merrill A. McPeak, "Don't Change 'Don't Ask, Don't Tell,'" *New York Times*, March 4, 2010. http://www.nytimes.com/2010/03/05/opinion/05mcpeak.html.

Dismissing the Common Arguments

None of the arguments for homosexuals serving openly have much merit if one understands the dynamics of small unit cohesion. The more common are easily dismissed:

- *Homosexuals have the same right to serve in uniform as heterosexuals.* This argument, supported by a number of conservatives, falsely asserts that military service is a right, rather than a privilege. The sole purpose of the military is to fight the country's wars; anything that undermines that purpose must be suppressed. The military rejects people for all sorts of reasons based on military effectiveness, and sexual preference is just one of many.

- *DADT [Don't Ask, Don't Tell] creates an atmosphere of deception.* Despite DADT, homosexual behavior is still a military offense (so is adultery). DADT merely prevented the military from actively searching for homosexuals in the ranks. If caught, they should not lie about it, but take the consequences of willfully violating the Uniform Code of Military Justice. The argument does not address the effects of open homosexuals on morale, readiness and combat effectiveness.
- *There is no evidence that homosexuality undermines morale or military effectiveness.* Several armies now allow homosexuals to serve openly—including the armies of Israel and the United Kingdom. But history provides plenty of evidence that homosexuality does undermine unit cohesion. The current practices of other armies are an experiment in progress, which should not overturn empirically proven policies. There are also significant differences between those armies and the United States military. The first is scale—the entire British army is barely the size of the Marine Corps, while the Israeli army is very small unless fully mobilized. Neither the British nor the Israeli armies undertake extended overseas deployments of the length or scale of the U.S. military; the Israeli army is very much a "commuter" force, with most troops living at home unless serving in the field—which is only an hour or so from home. As a result, neither has any experience with homosexuals serving in the field for extended periods. Finally, neither the British nor the Israeli armies have experienced anything approaching an extended, high-intensity war, so neither has any idea what effect homosexuals in the ranks might have on combat effectiveness.
- *The U.S. military needs the skills of homosexual soldiers.* Proponents of repeal always bring forth the gay Arabic linguist or battlefield surgeon who has been released from duty. It is implied that our anti-

quated policies are depriving the military of valuable personnel. Perhaps. The benefits of retaining them have to be weighed against the greater cost to combat effectiveness. Moreover, as homosexuals comprise only some 2.5% of the population, the numbers with which we are dealing are not statistically significant.

- *Allowing homosexuals to serve is the same as the fight to allow blacks to serve.* This is perhaps the most obnoxious and misleading canard of all. The differences ought to be obvious: race is superficial, while sexuality is ontological; i.e., race affects how one looks, sex and sexuality affect how one behaves. Blacks rightly reject the comparison, and so should the rest of us.

Opponents of gays in the military say that small-unit cohesion and combat effectiveness are at risk when gays serve openly.

Using the Military for Social Experiments

Military professionals ought to know that both allowing women to serve in combat and homosexuals to serve openly, undermine military effectiveness by injecting sexual dynamics into primary group relations. So far, the United States has not paid for its policy of allowing women to serve in positions that increasingly expose them to combat. The U.S. military has not really been tested against a first-rate adversary since the Vietnam war, and we do not know how well our units would perform under pressure from competent opposition in extended combat. We have no idea what effect gays serving openly will have, but we have every reason to believe it will be far more disruptive than either racial integration or the expansion of the role of women. But given that we are at war, do we really want to use the military as a laboratory for social experiments?

Analyze the essay:

1. To make his point, Stuart Koehl lays out five arguments for letting gay soldiers serve openly. Then, he knocks them down, one by one. Did you think this was an effective device with which to make his argument? Why or why not?
2. Koehl suggests that barring homosexuals from military service is not at all like barring African Americans from military service. In two to three sentences, explain what he means by this. Then, state your opinion on the matter. Do you think putting limits on people on the basis of their race is similar to putting restrictions on people because of their sexual orientation? Why or why not? Or, does it vary based on the situation?

Allowing Gay Soldiers to Serve Openly Protects Them from Harm

Viewpoint Three

Joseph Rocha

In the following essay Joseph Rocha argues that policies that prevent gay soldiers from serving openly contribute to gay soldiers' abuse by other military personnel. Rocha recounts how other soldiers humiliated and abused him when he served in the navy because they suspected he was gay. But because it was against the law to admit he was gay, Rocha was alone and unprotected—no law or policy made the abuse illegal. He contends that allowing gay soldiers to serve openly would protect them from such abuse. It would make it illegal and unacceptable to harass them, and it would give abused soldiers a system through which they could defend themselves. For all these reasons, Rocha concludes that allowing gay soldiers to serve openly protects them from abuse and harm.

Rocha served in the US Navy before being discharged for his sexuality.

Consider the following questions:

1. Who is chief petty officer Michael Toussaint and what did he order the author to do?
2. How many incidents of misconduct and abuse did the navy confirm took place in the author's unit?
3. What, according to Rocha, was the lowest point in his ordeal?

Joseph Rocha, "'Don't Ask, Don't Tell' Didn't Protect Me from Abuse in the Navy," *The Washington Post*, October 11, 2009. Copyright © 2009, Joseph Rocha. All rights reserved. Reproduced by permission.

I was 18 years old when I landed in the kingdom of Bahrain, off the coast of Saudi Arabia, in the winter of 2005. It was the first time I'd ever left the continental United States. My joints ached after more than 24 hours of travel, but I knew that a new life of service and adventure awaited me on the other side of that aircraft door.

Service Before Personal Life

This was the day I had been dreaming about since I'd enlisted in the Navy a few months before, on my birthday. I loved my country, and I knew that I was ready to prove myself in action.

I also knew that I was gay.

However, I chose to put service above my personal life. My understanding of the "don't ask, don't tell" policy was that if I kept quiet about my sexuality and didn't break any rules, I would face no punishment. I was wrong.

Once I joined the Navy, I was tormented by my chief and fellow sailors, physically and emotionally, for being gay. The irony of "don't ask, don't tell" is that it protects bigots and punishes gays who comply. Now, after a Youth Radio investigation of the abuses I suffered, the chief of naval operations ordered a thorough study of how the Navy handled the situation and is currently reviewing the document. I'm hopeful that the case will be reopened and top leadership finally held accountable for the lives they have ruined.

A Twenty-Eight-Month Nightmare

Within days of arriving at my duty station in Bahrain, I decided that I wanted to earn a place among the elite handlers working with dogs trained to detect explosives. After passing exams and completing training, I went from serving among hundreds of military police to serving in a specialized unit of two dozen handlers and 32 dogs. I was responsible for training and working with two dogs

Joseph Rocha joined an elite unit of dog handlers in charge of dogs trained to find explosives and improvised explosive devices (IEDs). He was harassed by fellow soldiers, who locked him in a feces-filled dog kennel because he admitted to being gay.

throughout the region. Our goal was to keep explosives and insurgents out of Iraq and Afghanistan.

For 12 hours a day in 112-degree heat with 85 percent humidity, we searched vehicles for explosives and responded to any threats. I loved the job, but there wasn't a day that went by when I wasn't completely miserable.

Shop talk in the unit revolved around sex, either the prostitute-filled parties of days past or the escapades my comrades looked forward to. They interpreted my silence

Thousands Were Discharged

About 13,500 openly gay, lesbian, and bisexual service persons were discharged from the US military since the Don't Ask, Don't Tell policy took effect in 1993.

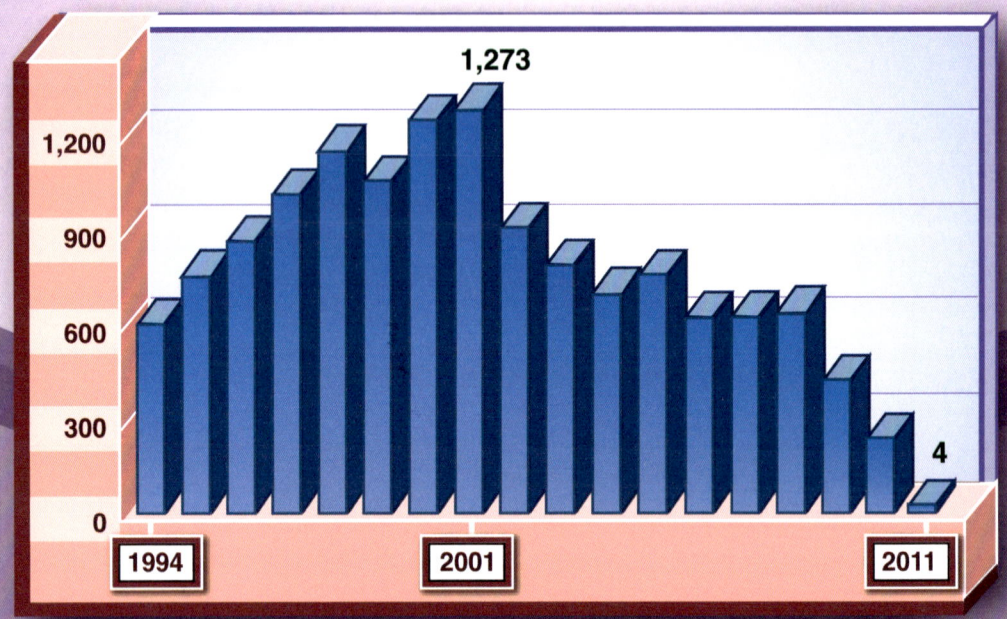

Note: All data except for 2009 includes the Coast Guard.

Taken from: Servicemembers Legal Defense Network, 2011.

and total lack of interest as an admission of homosexuality. My higher-ups seemed to think that gave them the right to bind me to chairs, ridicule me, hose me down and lock me in a feces-filled dog kennel.

I can't say for certain when the abuse started or when it stopped. Now, several years removed from those days in Bahrain, it blends together in my mind as a 28-month nightmare.

Ongoing Abuse and Humiliation

Once, the abuse was an all-day event; a training scenario turned into an excuse to humiliate me. Normally we ran the dogs through practice situations—an earthquake, a bomb or a fight—that we might encounter in our work. That day, in a classroom at an American school in Bahrain, with posters of the Founding Fathers lining the walls, the scenario happened to be me. I was the decoy, and I had to do just what Chief Petty Officer Michael Toussaint ordered.

In one corner of the classroom was a long sofa, turned away from the door. When you walked into the room, it appeared that one man was sitting on it, alone. But I was there too—the chief had decided that I would be down on my hands and knees, simulating oral sex. A kennel support staff member and I were supposed to pretend that we were in our bedroom and that the dogs were catching us having sex. Over and over, with each of the 32 dogs, I was forced to enact this scenario.

I told no one about what I was living through. I feared that reporting the abuse would lead to an investigation into my sexuality. My leaders and fellow sailors were punishing me for keeping my sexuality to myself, punishing me because I wouldn't "tell."

Left Tied Up in a Dog Kennel

I even saw "don't ask, don't tell" used against heterosexual female service members who had reported being the victims of sexual assault. If my chief acted on their statements, he would be forced to punish a friend of his, so the easiest way to make the problem go away was to scare the women into silence by saying something like: "You weren't sexually assaulted by a male in my unit. I hear you're a lesbian." After all, homosexuals have no rights in our military. You can't sexually assault someone who doesn't exist.

But the abuse wasn't invisible to everyone. In 2005, roughly six months into my time with that unit, a new sailor in our group was taken aback when I was left tied up in a dog kennel. She reported the incident and, from what I understand, this prompted an internal investigation into hazing in my unit. Even then, the abuse continued, and I still couldn't bring myself to talk about it. It took 90 minutes and the threat of a subpoena to get me to testify.

The Navy confirmed 93 incidents of misconduct, including hazing, abuse, physical assault, solicitation of prostitutes and misuse of government property and funds, but the case was closed. After receiving a letter of caution, the military's version of a slap on the wrist, my chief was eventually promoted in rank and position.

> ## DADT Threatens Soldiers and Their Families
>
> DADT puts gay people, their partners and their children at great risk for harm and blackmail. . . . Thousands [of] lesbian, gay and bisexual servicemembers still face the paralyzing dread that in a moment, their livelihood could vanish.
>
> Daniel Redman and Ilona Turner, "Don't Ask, Don't Tell—Anyone, Anywhere," *Nation*, November 16, 2010. http://www.thenation.com/article/156477/dont-ask-dont-tell—anyone-anywhere.

A Tragic Death

In the course of that investigation, the Navy decided to charge my best friend, Petty Officer 1st Class Jennifer Valdivia, a 27-year-old Sailor of the Year and second in command of my unit, for failing to put an end to my chief's tyranny. The idea that she could have stopped the abuse is, to me, unfair and unreasonable. The Navy itself failed to stop him.

Val, as I called her, was set to return home when she was told of the charges and that she wouldn't be leaving Bahrain as planned. She was afraid that she would never see the United States again. My mentor ended up taking her [own] life.

This incredible woman, whom I ate lunch with every Sunday and ran with every morning, was gone. Since the night I learned of her death, I have been haunted by nightmares. In my dreams, she's decomposing and suggests that the only way for me to stop my abuse is to follow her lead and end my life.

Just two days before she killed herself, Val gave me a gift, a token of congratulations on being accepted to the Naval Academy prep school in Rhode Island.

A Proud Officer Resigns

And despite everything that had happened—the abuse and her death—I decided to enroll. I wanted to put what had happened in Bahrain behind me. I had applied to the academy twice before I was finally accepted to the prep school, an education that would put me on my way to a commission from Annapolis.

It was my dream come true. I left Bahrain as a petty officer 3rd class and completed a six-week officer candidate boot camp. My commanders told me they wanted me to have a leadership role at the school. But after more than two years of abuse, the suicide of a fine sailor and the Navy's unwillingness to punish the top leadership in my unit, I was mentally and emotionally depleted. I refused to be punished any longer for who I am, so I made the most difficult decision of my life. I stood outside the office of my commanding officer with my knees buckling. My resignation read:

> I am a homosexual. I deeply regret that my personal feelings are not compatible with Naval regulations or policy. I am proud of my service and had hoped I would be able to serve the Navy and the country for my entire career. However, the principles of honor, courage and commitment mean I must be honest with myself, courageous in my beliefs, and committed in my action. I understand that this statement will be used to end my Naval career.

It would take two months for the Naval Academy and its lawyers to figure out what to do with me. The lawyers dove into a mess of technicalities. The "don't ask, don't tell" policy is riddled with inconsistencies, loopholes, unfairness and hypocrisy. As an officer candidate, I found

The US Congress voted to repeal the Don't Ask, Don't Tell policy in December 2010, which took effect in September 2011.

the situation even more confusing. Lawyers debated: Should they be consulting the "don't ask, don't tell" policy for officers or the regulations for enlisted personnel? Given the amount of money invested in military officers, the policy for them is far more forgiving.

A Dream Forfeited

During those weeks I was ordered to restricted duty and living quarters. I was stuck pulling weeds in the courtyard of the school, as students who had been my peers walked to class in their proud midshipmen-candidate uniforms. I was ordered not to contact my former classmates by any means. The school didn't want me to "influence them." This was my lowest point. Based on principle, based on dignity, I had forfeited my dream of a Naval Academy graduation.

Thankfully, I was discharged honorably with full benefits. Otherwise, I would have been left with no money for college and no health-care options for the severe depression, insomnia and post-traumatic stress disorder that Veterans Affairs physicians have diagnosed in me since I've returned from overseas. That [denial of benefits] would have been lawful under "don't ask, don't tell."

Serving with Security and Dignity

For years, I kept this story a secret from my loved ones, wanting simply to move on. But I believe we have a window of opportunity now in the effort to repeal "don't ask, don't tell," and this has propelled me to go public with my experience. This weekend [in October 2009], I will be at the National Equality March for gay rights in Washington, after traveling across the country speaking at gay pride events and at universities, trying to build momentum for a strategy for repeal.[1]

I'm doing all of this during midterms at the University of San Diego, where I am a junior majoring in political science. While my greatest regret is that I will never graduate from Annapolis, I am confident that soon I will serve proudly as a commissioned officer.

I don't think I will ever feel as powerless as I did when I was on my knees, wearing a U.S. military uniform in the Middle East, forced by my superior to shove my head between another man's legs. But I have discovered that telling this story holds its own kind of power.

The more I talk about what happened to me, the more I hear from others who have been in similar situations.

---

1. The US Congress repealed the Don't Ask, Don't Tell policy in December 2010, which went into effect on September 20, 2011.

Students in the service academies calling me, crying, asking if they should quit. World War II veterans. Enlisted soldiers serving overseas. They are hopeful that we may soon have a different kind of military, that gay and lesbian men and women can serve the country we love with job security and dignity.

Despite everything, I am hopeful, too.

Analyze the essay:

1. Instead of relying on facts, statistics, or historical examples the way other essays in this section do to make their arguments, this essay primarily focuses on Joseph Rocha's personal experiences as a gay sailor. In what ways does this style differ? What advantages and disadvantages might there be in describing a personal story to make an argument about a topic like gays in the military? Explain your answer thoroughly, citing at least one advantage and one disadvantage.

2. In this essay the author claims that forcing gay soldiers to serve in the closet encourages their abuse and renders them powerless. How do you think each of the other authors in this section might respond to this claim? List each speaker and write two to three sentences on what you think their response might be.

Allowing Gay Soldiers to Serve Openly Puts Them at Risk

Viewpoint Four

Eric Harbin

Eric Harbin wrote this essay when he was a student at California State University, Northridge. In it, he argues that policies preventing gay soldiers from serving openly protect them from harm and abuse. Gay soldiers whose sexuality is not known cannot be abused, says Harbin. On the other hand, if gay soldiers are open about their sexuality, they can—and will—become a target of abuse. He explains that much of America, including the military, is intolerant. Allowing gays to serve openly would single them out, drawing attention to their homosexuality, which Harbin thinks would cause them to become targets of abuse. Harbin hopes that one day such intolerance and bigotry can be overcome but suggests the military is not yet ready for openly gay soldiers. He concludes that society at large must do more to combat homophobia and intolerance before the military will be capable of peacefully accepting homosexuals into its ranks.

Consider the following questions:
1. How many hate crimes does Harbin say are committed because of the victim's sexual orientation?
2. Who was Petty Officer Allen R. Schindler Jr., and how does he factor into the author's argument?
3. What does the word *symptom* mean as used by Harbin?

Eric Harbin, "Too Soon to End 'Don't Ask, Don't Tell,'" *Daily Sundial* (California State University, Northridge), October 4, 2010. Sundial.csun.edu. All rights reserved. Reproduced by permission.

Congress was correct in upholding the "don't ask, don't tell" [DADT] policy [in October 2010].[1] Although gay rights activists are continuing the fight to get the policy repealed, it is important to take into consideration the inadvertent repercussions of the policy's removal.

It could endanger our homosexual troops and would only cure a symptom of the discrimination problem in America.

DADT Keeps Gay Soldiers Safe

Instead of hastily repealing "don't ask, don't tell," we need to first eradicate homophobia and discrimination from American society.

It is important to keep in mind the safety of our homosexual troops when discussing "don't ask, don't tell."

Our campus [California State University, Northridge (CSUN)] is a very open and safe environment for people of all cultures, races, and sexual orientations. However, not all places are as accepting as CSUN.

According to data released by the FBI in 2008, one out of every six hate crimes are because of sexual orientation.

In the same report, the FBI reported there was an 11 percent increase in sexual orientation–motivated crimes from 2007 to 2008.

If a military professional were openly gay, it could put them in immediate physical harm and could increase the number of hate crimes committed against them.

There would also be emotional consequences to homosexuals serving

---

Openly Gay Soldiers Will Be Attacked by Straight Soldiers

In basic training, where all members of the services enter in, they are sequestered together in close quarters. They sleep side by side, and yes even shower together. I remember being in a shower with 20 other guys in basic training and actually feeling nothing of uncomfortableness. But then I wasn't aware if in my midst there was anybody gay there with us. Again you may suspect, but you just didn't know. However I could tell you that if there had been and it [had] been known, it wouldn't have been pretty. PC [political correctness] aside, it's just the fact of the situation. There would have been blood.

Mac Ranger, "The Peril of Repealing DADT—There Will Be Blood," *MacRanger Radio Show Blog*, Macsmind.com, December 19, 2010. http://macsmind.com/wordpress/2010/12/19/the-peril-of-of-repealing-dadt-there-will-be-blood/.

---

1. This position was later reversed in December 2010, when Don't Ask, Don't Tell was repealed and went into law on September 20, 2011.

openly in the military. Homosexuals could be discriminated against by commanding officers, subjected to verbal slurs from other soldiers, and may be less likely to receive assistance in combat.

The original reason the "don't ask, don't tell" policy was put into place was to protect homosexual soldiers.

In 1992, Petty Officer Allen R. Schindler Jr. was beaten and murdered by his fellow shipmates because he was openly gay.

Former President [Bill] Clinton used this brutal murder as an example when passing the policy.

Although any hate crime should not be tolerated, if the "don't ask, don't tell" policy is repealed, it could lead to more crimes such as this.

Though proponents of DADT warn reversing the policy will put gay service members at risk, in November 2010 the Pentagon concluded that repealing DADT would do more good than harm.

The Military Depends on Uniformity

The military creates an environment that impedes individualism in favor of uniformity. This is why there are uniforms and specific hair cuts that soldiers must have—to maintain consistency.

Don't Ask, Don't Tell Kept Gay Soldiers Safe

A 2010 poll of active duty military found the majority thought that Don't Ask, Don't Tell helped protect gay and lesbian soldiers from harassment, violence, and hate crimes.

Question: "How effective is the Don't Ask, Don't Tell policy at reducing violence and hate crimes against gay personnel?"

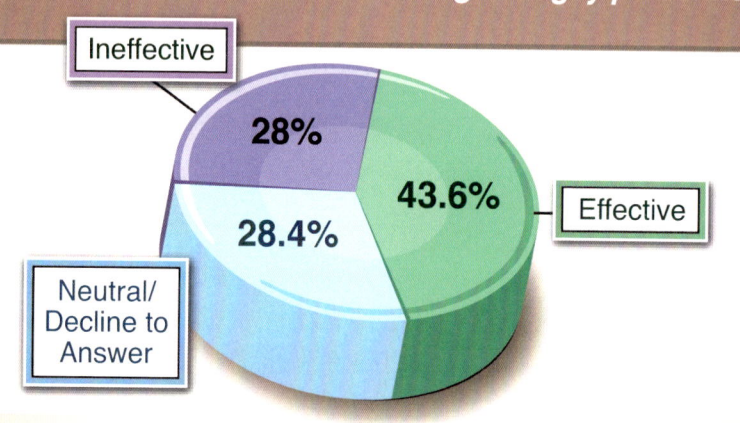

- Ineffective: 28%
- Neutral/Decline to Answer: 28.4%
- Effective: 43.6%

Question: "How effective is the Don't Ask, Don't Tell policy at reducing harassment against gay personnel?"

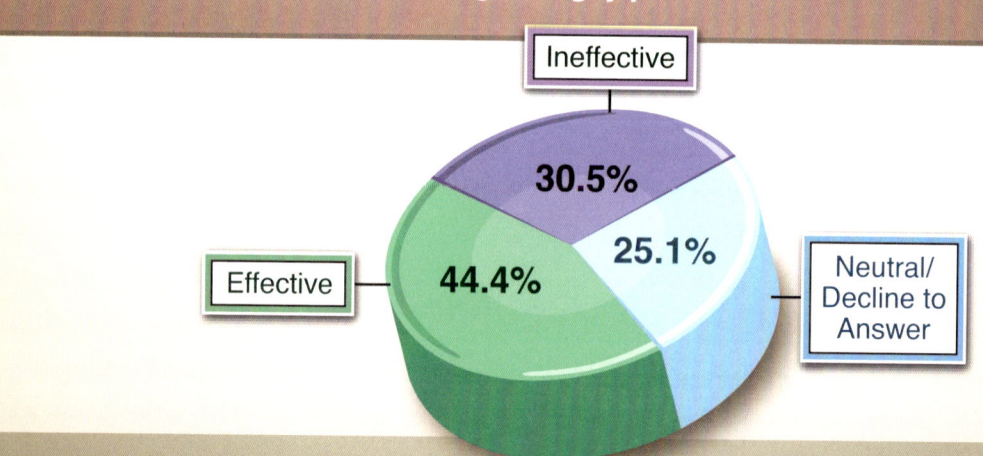

- Ineffective: 30.5%
- Neutral/Decline to Answer: 25.1%
- Effective: 44.4%

Taken from: "Don't Ask, Don't Tell" Survey Results (Active Duty), *Military Times*, 2010.

General James Amos, assistant commander of the US Marine Corps, testifies before Congress in November 2010. He argued that repealing DADT could put gay service members at risk.

Openly gay soldiers would be singling themselves out from the group. This puts gay troops at risk to be the targets of discrimination or violence.

In a perfect world, people of all sexual orientations should be able to work and fight together in the military without fear of persecution.

However, in the current social and military environments, it is unrealistic to expect openly gay people to be embraced in the military.

Society Must Change Before the Military Does

Instead of fighting against the "don't ask, don't tell" policy, we should be working to change the mentality of American society to embrace all sexual orientations.

We need to educate our children to be accepting and eradicate homophobia so that, when they are old enough to serve in the military, sexual orientation will not even be an issue.

I disagree with the idea that homosexuality is incompatible with military service, which is the reason that Former President [Ronald] Reagan didn't allow homosexuals to serve in the military.

Homosexual soldiers are just as capable of serving in our military as heterosexual soldiers.

However, in our current social climate, it would be irresponsible to repeal the policy of "don't ask, don't tell."

By repealing the policy at this stage in our history, it would do more damage than good.

It would endanger our gay troops, and would just be removing a symptom of the real problem in America: homophobia and discrimination. Change comes slowly, and instead of opening our gay troops up for violence and abuse, we must strive for equality in all aspects of American culture.

Analyze the essay:

1. Unlike some of the other authors in this section, the author of this essay thinks that homosexuality is compatible with military service and is upset that homophobia is a problem in American society. Does it surprise you that someone who thinks this would argue in support of a policy like Don't Ask, Don't Tell? Why or why not?
2. What parts of Eric Harbin's essay are opinions? What parts are facts? Make a list of opinions and facts and see which the author relies on more to make his argument.

Allowing Gays to Serve Openly Will Strengthen the US Military

Viewpoint Five

Stephen Benjamin

In the following essay Stephen Benjamin argues that when gay soldiers are dismissed from service, the military loses badly needed talented and skilled personnel. He explains that for years, the military has suffered from a shortage of trained and qualified soldiers. Yet thousands of soldiers who hold critical jobs in language translation, medicine, counterterrorism, and other fields have been kicked out of the military because of their sexual orientation. In Benjamin's opinion, this practice is a great disservice to all Americans because the military becomes less functional and Americans become less safe. Benjamin believes that a soldier's skills are more important than his or her sexual orientation. He concludes that the military should benefit from the most skilled and qualified Americans, regardless of their sexual orientation.

Benjamin is a former petty officer second class. He was dismissed from the navy in 2006 because he is gay.

Consider the following questions:

1. How many Arabic linguists does Benjamin say have been kicked out of the military because of their sexual orientation?
2. What kinds of jobs did some of the eleven thousand dismissed gay soldiers hold according to Benjamin?
3. How many soldiers does the author say might be added to the military's ranks following Don't Ask, Don't Tell's repeal?

Stephen Benjamin, "Don't Ask, Don't Translate," *The New York Times*, June 6, 2007. Copyright © 2007 by The New York Times. All rights reserved. Reproduced by permission.

Active and non-active gay military personnel march in a gay pride parade after the announcement of the repeal of Don't Ask, Don't Tell. Many people contend that dropping the policy will strengthen the US military.

Imagine for a moment an American soldier deep in the Iraqi desert. His unit is about to head out when he receives a cable detailing an insurgent ambush right in his convoy's path. With this information, he and his soldiers are now prepared for the danger that lies ahead.

Reports like these are regularly sent from military translators' desks, providing critical, often life-saving intelligence to troops fighting in Iraq and Afghanistan. But the military has a desperate shortage of linguists trained to translate such invaluable information and convey it to the war zone.

The lack of qualified translators has been a pressing issue for some time—the Army had filled only half its authorized positions for Arabic translators in 2001. Cables went untranslated on Sept. 10 that might have prevented the terrorist attacks on Sept. 11. Today, the American Embassy in Baghdad has nearly 1,000 personnel, but only a handful of fluent Arabic speakers.

I was an Arabic translator. After joining the Navy in 2003, I attended the Defense Language Institute, graduated in the top 10 percent of my class and then spent two years giving our troops the critical translation services they desperately needed. I was ready to serve in Iraq.

But I never got to. In March, I was ousted from the Navy under the "don't ask, don't tell" policy, which mandates dismissal if a service member is found to be gay.

Dismissed Because He Is Gay

My story begins almost a year ago [in 2006] when my roommate, who is also gay, was deployed to Fallujah [Iraq]. We communicated the only way we could: using the military's instant-messaging system on monitored government computers. These electronic conversations are lifelines, keeping soldiers sane while mortars land meters away.

Then, last October [2006] the annual inspection of my base, Fort Gordon, Ga., included a perusal of the government computer chat system; inspectors identified 70 service members whose use violated policy. The range of violations was broad: people were flagged for everything from profanity to outright discussions of explicit sexual activity. Among those charged were my former roommate and me. Our messages had included references to our social lives—comments that were otherwise unremarkable, except that they indicated we were both gay.

Discharging Gay Soldiers Robs the Military of Highly Skilled People

Although [DADT] humiliated and ruined the careers of many soldiers, Arabic linguists suffered disproportionately at a time when their skills were indispensable. By adhering to the policy—especially during wartime—three Presidential administrations handicapped American military capability and demonstrated the policy not only inhumane but self-defeating.

Sasha Suderow, "Don't Ask Don't Tell: A Story Highlighting the Anguish Faced by Soldiers with Indispensable Skills," *Huffington Post*, March 12, 2010. www.huffingtonpost.com/sasha-suderow/dont-ask-dont-tell-a-stor_b_496565.html.

Openly Gay Soldiers Would Not Weaken the US Military

A 2010 Quinnipiac University poll found that the majority of Americans surveyed do not think letting gay soldiers serve openly would negatively affect troops' ability to fight.

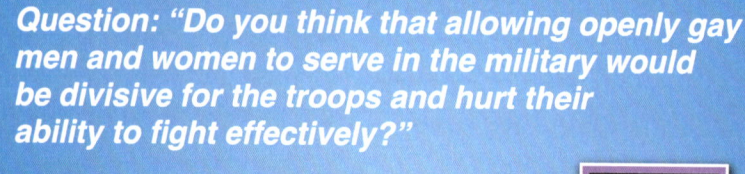

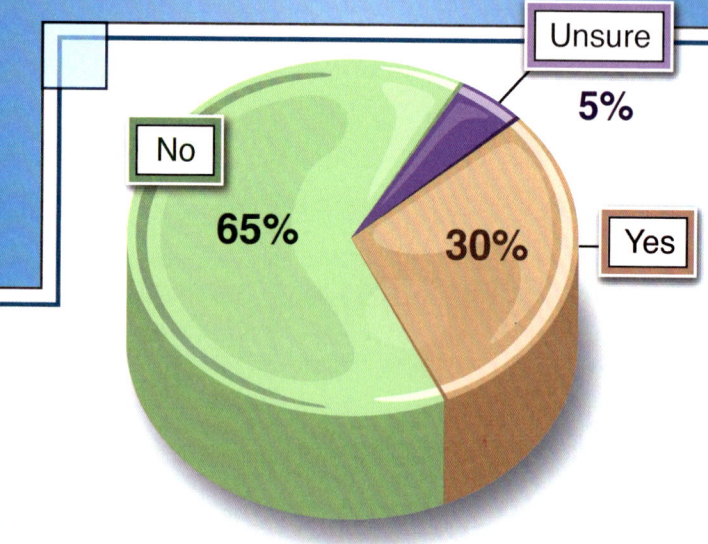

Question: "Do you think that allowing openly gay men and women to serve in the military would be divisive for the troops and hurt their ability to fight effectively?"

- No: 65%
- Yes: 30%
- Unsure: 5%

Taken from: Quinnipiac University Poll, February 2–8, 2010.

I could have written a statement denying that I was homosexual, but lying did not seem like the right thing to do. My roommate made the same decision, though he was allowed to remain in Iraq until the scheduled end of his tour.

The result was the termination of our careers, and the loss to the military of two more Arabic translators. The 68 other—heterosexual—service members remained on active duty, despite many having committed violations far more egregious than ours; the Pentagon apparently doesn't consider hate speech, derogatory comments about women or sexual misconduct grounds for dismissal.

Depriving the Military of Badly Needed Talent

My supervisors did not want to lose me. Most of my peers knew I was gay, and that didn't bother them. I was always accepted as a member of the team. And my experience was not anomalous: polls of veterans from Iraq and Afghanistan show an overwhelming majority are comfortable with gays. Many were aware of at least one gay person in their unit and had no problem with it.

The US military's policy toward gays curtailed its abilities to recruit and train Arabic translators. Many Arabic translators who were gay were discharged from the military.

"Don't ask, don't tell" does nothing but deprive the military of talent it needs and invade the privacy of gay service members just trying to do their jobs and live their lives. Political and military leaders who support the current law may believe that homosexual soldiers threaten unit cohesion and military readiness, but the real damage is caused by denying enlistment to patriotic Americans and wrenching qualified individuals out of effective military units. This does not serve the military or the nation well.

Consider: more than 58 Arabic linguists have been kicked out since "don't ask, don't tell" was instituted. How much valuable intelligence could those men and women be providing today to troops in harm's way?

In addition to those translators, 11,000 other service members have been ousted since the "don't ask, don't tell" policy was passed by Congress in 1993. Many held critical jobs in intelligence, medicine and counterterrorism. An untold number of closeted gay military members don't re-enlist because of the pressure the law puts on them. This is the real cost of the ban—and, with our military so overcommitted and undermanned, it's too high to pay.

Ready, Waiting—and Barred from Service

In response to difficult recruiting prospects, the Army has already taken a number of steps, lengthening soldiers' deployments to 15 months from 12, enlisting felons and extending the age limit to 42. Why then won't Congress pass a bill like the Military Readiness Enhancement Act, which would repeal "don't ask, don't tell"? The bipartisan bill, by some analysts' estimates, could add more than 41,000 soldiers—all gay, of course.

As the friends I once served with head off to 15-month deployments, I regret I'm not there to lessen their burden and to serve my country. I'm trained to fight, I speak Arabic and I'm willing to serve. No recruiter needs to make a persuasive argument to sign me up. I'm ready, and I'm waiting.

Analyze the essay:

1. In this essay Stephen Benjamin uses facts, statistics, and personal experience to argue that gay soldiers improve the quality of the US military. He does not, however, use any quotations to support his point. If you were to rewrite this article and insert quotations, what authorities might you quote from? Where would you place the quotations, and why?

2. Benjamin contends that America is in dire need of skilled soldiers who can speak and read Arabic. How does Stuart Koehl, author of Viewpoint Two in this section, respond to this argument? After considering both arguments, with which author do you ultimately agree: Benjamin or Koehl? Why? Name at least one piece of evidence that swayed you.

Viewpoint Six

Allowing Gays to Serve Openly Will Weaken the US Military

Robert G. Marshall

Robert G. Marshall is a Republican who serves in Virginia's state legislature. In the following essay he warns that allowing gays to serve openly in the military will critically threaten the military's effectiveness. Some gay soldiers might enlist if they are allowed to serve openly, but Marshall says thousands of straight soldiers will leave because they do not want to serve with gay people. This circumstance will weaken the US military and deprive it of very talented people, he warns. Furthermore, Marshall suggests that foreigners who cooperate with the US military—many of whom are from societies that view homosexuality as immoral, even evil—will no longer want to help the United States, further weakening the military. Finally, Marshall warns that homosexuals pose a health threat to straight soldiers. For all of these reasons he concludes that gays should not be allowed to serve openly in the military and that allowing them to do so undermines national security.

Consider the following questions:

1. What percentage of marine combat troops does Marshall say would leave the military early if gays were allowed to serve openly?
2. What percentage of army combat troops think the presence of openly gay soldiers would negatively affect their ability to do their job, according to the author?
3. What health risk do gay soldiers pose to straight soldiers, in Marshall's opinion?

Robert G. Marshall, "DADT Repeal Threatens Morals, Morale," *Daily Press*, January 8, 2011. www.dailypress.com. All rights reserved. Reproduced by permission.

President Barack Obama had little time before the arrival of the newly elected Congress to repeal "Don't act, don't tell" [DADT]. The measure was tacked onto a Small Business Technology bill with little debate and no amendments and passed the weekend before Christmas [2010] by a "lame duck" Congress, ending 232 years of military policy dating back to George Washington, and 6,000 years of moral tradition.

Sen. Joe Lieberman cited the Declaration of Independence. Sen. Harry Reid said repeal of DADT was the ideal of the Founders. The vote was hailed as a victory for "tolerance." Our Founders didn't pledge their "lives, their fortunes and their sacred honor" to protect behavior which was a felony.

Straight Soldiers Do Not Want to Serve with Gay Soldiers

Our military exists to protect our country. The Pentagon study of DADT admitted that, "Our sense is that the majority of views expressed were against repeal." How will ignoring troops' opinions affect morale?

Of Marine combat troops, 32 percent would leave early if DADT were repealed. Another 16.2 percent would consider [leaving]. For Army combat troops, 21.4 percent would leave and 14.6 percent would consider it. This decline could endanger remaining troops, compromise foreign policy and precipitate a compulsory military draft. No foreign enemy could have delivered a more devastating blow.

Another 48.9 percent of Army and 59.7 percent of Marine combat troops say repeal of DADT would negatively affect trust; 47.5 percent of Army and 57.5 percent of Marine combat troops said repeal would negatively affect their ability to get the job done.

Gay Soldiers Undermine Military Morality

The moral element is the most critical element in any fighting unit. The threat of mass departure of troops

Countries That Allow Openly Gay Citizens to Serve in the Military

More than twenty-five countries allow gay soldiers to openly serve in their military.

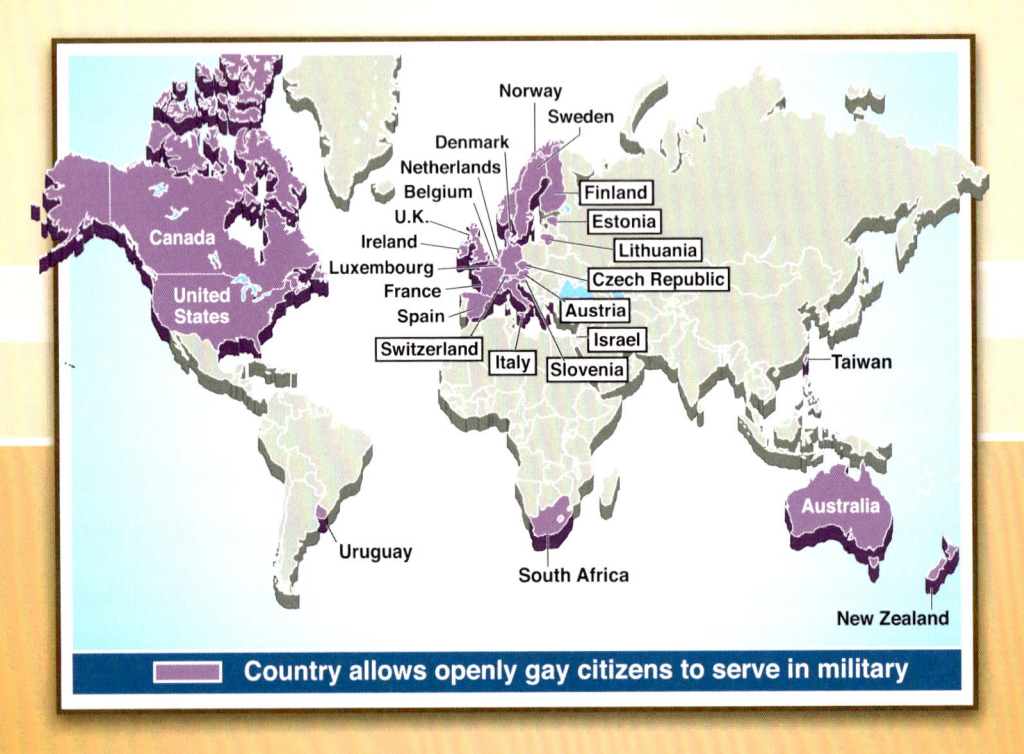

Country allows openly gay citizens to serve in military

Countries labeled on map: Canada, United States, Uruguay, Norway, Sweden, Denmark, Netherlands, Belgium, U.K., Ireland, Luxembourg, France, Spain, Switzerland, Italy, Finland, Estonia, Lithuania, Czech Republic, Austria, Israel, Slovenia, South Africa, Taiwan, Australia, New Zealand.

* The United States repealed its policy prohibiting gays from serving openly in 2010, and the repeal became law in September 2011.

Taken from: University of California, Santa Barbara, Palm Center, June 2009.

must be taken seriously. Is it just a coincidence that the Pentagon is now announcing significant future manpower reductions at the same time many of our troops said they will not reenlist under these radical new terms?

Military chaplains overwhelmingly supported racial integration of the armed services. But chaplains overwhelmingly oppose repeal of DADT. Most troops oppose repeal for religious and moral reasons. The Pentagon's response to 6,000 years of moral teaching is "attitude restructuring courses."

Will our Muslim Pakistani allies who oppose homosexual behavior eagerly help us keep the Taliban from securing chemical and nuclear weapons?

This DADT repeal is an untested social experiment and will be used to attack state constitution marriage amendments and push the homosexual agenda into schools.

President Obama said homosexuals lived a "lie" under DADT. But who is propagating a lie by ignoring volumes of peer-reviewed social science and medical literature confirming vast differences between heterosexual and homosexual relationships regarding duration of commitment, number of partners, violence and health risks as confirmed by homosexual-advocacy literature?

Although the FDA [Food and Drug Administration] prohibits men who have sex with men from donating blood, the surgeon generals of the military services concluded there were no additional risks for blood contact and battlefield transfusions from persons who engage in the very behavior that spreads AIDS and other pathologies. The Pentagon report nevertheless recommends decriminalizing consensual sodomy.

> **Allowing Gays to Serve Will Generate Anti-US Sentiment**
>
> All major religions teach the primacy of sex between husbands and wives and the immorality of homosexuality. Enforcing acceptance of homosexuality may endear us to the weak sisters of Western Europe, but it puts the United States military in conflict with universal moral traditions. Between this and Hollywood, it shouldn't be hard for our enemies to make an even stronger case that we're 'the Great Satan.'"
>
> Robert Knight, "A New Meaning for 'Brothers in Arms,'" *Washington Times*, December 20, 2010. www.washingtontimes.com/news/2010/dec/20/a-new-meaning-for-brothers-in-arms/ ?page = l.

The Military Must Have Standards

Because the Virginia National Guard is separate from the U.S. Army Reserve, I will introduce a bill to maintain the Guard's DADT policy. Virginia imposes different enlistment standards (with or without waivers) for the National Guard than Congress does for the armed forces in the areas of driving infractions, education and drug convictions.

President Barack Obama signs legislation to end the Don't Ask, Don't Tell policy. Thirty-two percent of marines and twenty one percent of army personnel said they would leave the military early if DADT were repealed.

Former U.S. Supreme Court Justice Joseph Story noted in his "Commentaries on the Constitution," "The power of the militia [now called National Guard] . . . was limited and concurrent with that of the States . . . The power to discipline and train the military, except when in the actual service of the United States, was also vested exclusively in the States, and under such circumstances was secure against any serious abuses."

Even liberal Supreme Court Justice John Paul Stevens said members of state Guard units wear "a civilian hat, a state militia hat, and an army hat—only one of which is worn at any particular time." (*Perpitch v. Dept. of Defense*, 1990)

Under DADT, orientation did not lead to discharge, behavior did. While all persons have inherent human dignity, we must scrutinize actions and uphold standards for the military and our nation.

Analyze the essay:

1. The author of this essay is a Republican politician. The author of the previous essay, Stephen Benjamin, is a former sailor who was dismissed from the navy because he is gay. Does knowing the backgrounds of these authors influence your opinion of their arguments? Are you more likely to side with one or the other because of his background? If not, why not? If so, in what way?
2. In this essay Robert G. Marshall maintains that allowing gay soldiers to serve openly will threaten the quality of the US military. What pieces of evidence does he provide to support this claim? List at least three. Do these convince you of his argument? Explain why or why not.

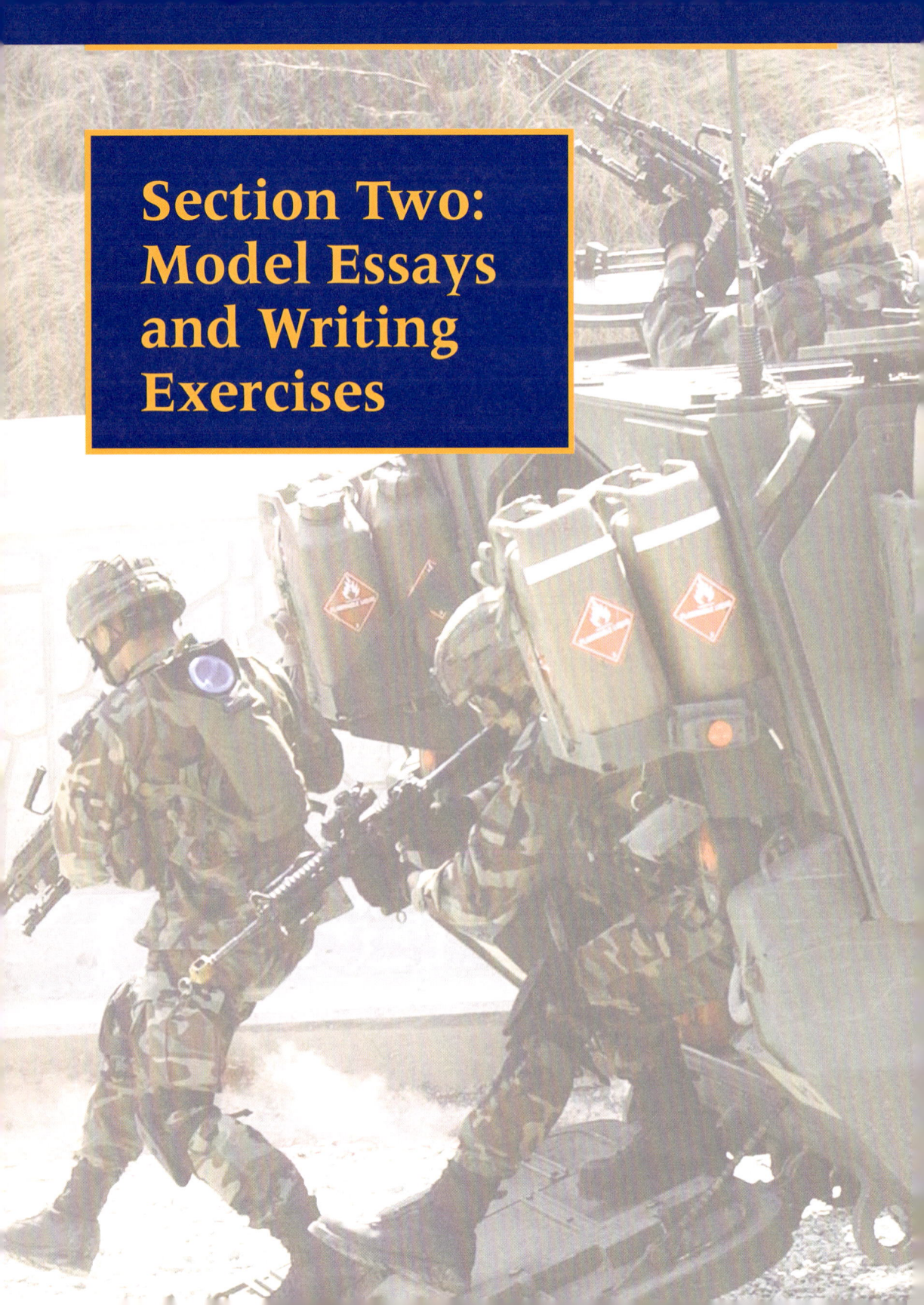

Section Two: Model Essays and Writing Exercises

The Five-Paragraph Essay

Preface A

An *essay* is a short piece of writing that discusses or analyzes one topic. The five-paragraph essay is a form commonly used in school assignments and tests. Every five-paragraph essay begins with an *introduction*, ends with a *conclusion*, and features three *supporting paragraphs* in the middle.

The Thesis Statement. The introduction includes the essay's thesis statement. The thesis statement presents the argument or point the author is trying to make about the topic. The essays in this book all have different thesis statements because they are making different arguments about gays in the military.

The thesis statement should clearly tell the reader what the essay will be about. A focused thesis statement helps determine what will be in the essay; the subsequent paragraphs are spent developing and supporting its argument.

The Introduction. In addition to presenting the thesis statement, a well-written introductory paragraph captures the attention of the reader and explains why the topic being explored is important. It may provide the reader with background information on the subject matter or feature an anecdote that illustrates a point relevant to the topic. It could also present startling information that clarifies the point of the essay or put forth a contradictory position that the essay will refute. Further techniques for writing an introduction are found later in this section.

The Supporting Paragraphs. The introduction is then followed by three (or more) supporting paragraphs. These are the main body of the essay. Each paragraph presents and develops a *subtopic* that supports the essay's thesis statement. Each subtopic is spearheaded by a *topic sentence* and supported by its own facts, details, and examples. The writer can use various kinds of supporting material and details to back up the topic of each supporting paragraph. These may include statistics, quotations from people with special knowledge or expertise, historic facts, and anecdotes. A rule of writing is that specific and concrete examples are more convincing than vague, general, or unsupported assertions.

The Conclusion. The conclusion is the paragraph that closes the essay. Its function is to summarize or reiterate the main idea of the essay. It may recall an idea from the introduction or briefly examine the larger implications of the thesis. Because the conclusion is also the last chance a writer has to make an impression on the reader, it is important that it not simply repeat what has been presented elsewhere in the essay but close it in a clear, final, and memorable way.

Although the order of the essay's component paragraphs is important, the paragraphs do not have to be written in the order presented here. Some writers like to decide on a thesis and write the introduction paragraph first. Other writers like to focus first on the body of the essay and write the introduction and conclusion later.

Pitfalls to Avoid

When writing essays about controversial issues such as gays in the military, it is important to remember that disputes over the material are common precisely because there are many different perspectives. Remember to state your arguments in careful and measured terms. Evaluate your topic fairly—avoid overstating negative qualities of one perspective or understating positive qualities of another. Use examples, facts, and details to support any assertions you make.

The Persuasive Essay

There are many types of essays, but in general, they are usually short compositions in which the writer expresses and discusses an opinion about something. In the persuasive essay the writer tries to persuade the reader to do something or to convince the reader to agree with the writer's opinion about something. Examples of persuasive writing are easy to find. Advertising is one common example. Through radio and TV commercials and print ads, companies try to convince the public to buy their products for specific reasons. A lot of everyday writing is persuasive, too. Letters to the editor, posts from sports fans on team blogs, even handwritten notes urging a friend to listen to a new CD—all are examples of persuasive writing.

The Tools of Persuasion

The writer of the persuasive essay uses various tools to persuade the reader. Here are some of them:

Facts and statistics. A fact is a statement that no one typically would disagree with. It can be verified by information in reputable resources such as encyclopedias, almanacs, government websites, or reference books about the topic of the fact.

Examples of Facts and Statistics

Valentine's Day is celebrated on February 14.
Bangkok is the capital of Thailand.
Eighty-two percent of Americans own a cell phone.
According to a CNN/Opinion Research Corporation poll, 87 percent of Americans thought the Gulf of Mexico had not completely recovered from the 2010 oil spill that occurred there.

It is important to note that facts and statistics can be *misstated* (written down or quoted incorrectly), *misinterpreted* (not understood correctly by the user), or *misused* (not used fairly). But, if a writer uses facts and statistics properly, they can add authority to the writer's essay.

Opinions. An opinion is what a person thinks about something. It can be contested or argued with; however, opinions of people who are experts on the topic or who have personal experience are often very convincing. Many persuasive essays are written to convince the reader that the writer's opinion is worth believing and acting on.

Testimonials. A testimonial is a statement given by a person who is thought to be an expert or who has another trait people admire, such as being a celebrity. Television commercials frequently use testimonials to convince watchers to buy the products they are advertising.

Examples. An example is something that is representative of a group or type ("penne" is an example of the group "pasta"). Examples are used to help define, describe, or illustrate something to make it more understandable.

Anecdotes. Anecdotes are extended examples. They are little stories with a beginning, middle, and end. They can be used just like examples to explain something or to show something about a topic.

Appeals to Reason. One way to convince readers that an opinion or action is right is to appeal to reason or logic. This often involves the idea that if some ideas are true, another must also be true. Here is an example of one type of appeal to reason:

— Eating fast food causes obesity and diabetes, just as smoking cigarettes causes lung cancer and asthma. For this reason, fast-food companies, like cigarette manufacturers, should be held legally responsible for their customers' health.

Appeals to Emotion. Another way to persuade readers to believe or do something is to appeal to their emotions—love, fear, pity, loyalty, and anger are some of the emotions to which writers appeal. A writer who wants to persuade someone not to eat meat might appeal to their love of animals:

— If you own a cat, dog, hamster, or bird, you should not eat meat. It makes no sense to pamper and love your pet while at the same time supporting the merciless slaughter of other animals for your dinner.

Ridicule and Name-Calling. Ridicule and name-calling are not good techniques to use in a persuasive essay. Instead of exploring the strengths of the topic, the writer who uses these relies on making those who oppose the main idea look foolish, evil, or stupid. In most cases, the writer who does this weakens his or her argument.

Bandwagon. The writer who uses the bandwagon technique appeals to the idea that "everybody thinks this or is doing this; therefore it is valid." The bandwagon method is not a very authoritative way to convince your reader of your point.

Words and Phrases Common to Persuasive Essays

accordingly	it stands to reason
because	it then follows that
clearly	obviously
consequently	since
for this reason	subsequently
indeed	therefore
in fact	this is why
it is necessary to	thus
it makes sense to	we must
it seems clear that	yet

Essay One

America's Confusion: Openly Gay Soldiers and Civil Rights in the Military

> **Editor's Notes** Persuasive essays typically try to get a reader to agree with the author's point of view. This is the goal of the following model essay. It argues that banning openly gay people from serving in the military is not a civil rights issue. The essay is structured as a five-paragraph essay in which each paragraph contributes a piece of evidence to develop the argument.
>
> The notes in the margin point out key features of the essay and will help you understand how the essay is organized. Also note that all sources are cited using Modern Language Association (MLA) style*. For more information on how to cite your sources see Appendix C. In addition, consider the following:
>
> 1. How does the introduction engage the reader's attention?
> 2. What persuasive techniques are used in the essay?
> 3. What purpose do the essay's quotes serve?
> 4. Does the essay convince you of its point?

- 🟩 Refers to thesis and topic sentences
- 🟨 Refers to supporting details

Paragraph 1

Critics of the "Don't Ask, Don't Tell" (DADT) policy frequently complain that preventing gays from serving openly in the military is a violation of their civil rights. This argument is well-intentioned but completely wrong. **Allowing gays to openly serve in the military is not a civil rights issue because the military is not a democracy, not**

This is the essay's thesis statement. It gets to the heart of the author's argument.

---

* Editor's Note: In applying MLA style guidelines in this book, the following simplifications have been made: Parenthetical text citations are confined to direct quotations only; electronic source documentation in the Works Cited list omits date of access, page ranges, and some detailed facts of publication.

64

everyone is fit for service, and gay soldiers are not barred from service.

Paragraph 2

That people should be granted full civil rights in civilian society is unquestionable; the hallmark of a democracy is that every citizen is afforded the same rights. Yet those who oppose DADT misunderstand that the military is *not* a democracy, nor should it be. Military life is quite different from civilian life in that soldiers, while on duty and in uniform, do not have the same rights as civilians. Soldiers are not free to express their beliefs, to dress how they want, or to engage in other simple behaviors that it would be unthinkable to restrict in civilian society. "The military is not a democracy," asserts Andy Martin, a conservative columnist who hopes to be elected US president in 2012. "We do not get to express our 'constitutional rights' in the military the same way we do in civilian life." (Martin) There are good reasons the military is not democratic. Military functionality depends on taking orders, obeying, and not questioning, interpreting, or veering from the plan: in other words, the very opposite of what occurs in a democracy. The idea that the military should reflect the democratic ideals of the civilian arena is incongruent with the military's very essence.

Paragraph 3

In addition to not being a democracy, the military is under no obligation to offer service to everyone. In fact, the military routinely disqualifies certain people for service, and for good reasons. "People cannot serve in uniform if they are too old or too young, too fat or too thin, too tall or too short, disabled, not sufficiently educated and so on," writes former air force chief of staff Merrill A. McPeak. (McPeak) People are turned away from military service all the time because they do not meet the military's specific criteria. In this way the military is unlike most other American employers, who are not allowed to discriminate when they hire. It is unfair to argue that the military should

This is the topic sentence of Paragraph 2. Note that all of the paragraph's details fit with, or support, it.

Note how this quote supports the ideas discussed in the paragraph. It also comes from a reputable source.

This is the topic sentence of Paragraph 3. Without reading the rest of the paragraph, take a guess at what the paragraph will be about.

"In fact" is a transitional phrase that helps keep the ideas in the essay flowing. Make a list of all transitional words and phrases used in the essay.

Why do you think the author has included Merrill A. McPeak's job title?

not be able to pick and choose the people with the qualities that best dispose them to the realities of military service.

Paragraph 4

Finally, although critics argue that the ban on openly gay soldiers is akin to the ban on African American soldiers' serving with white soldiers until the mid-twentieth century, in truth the two are not at all similar. African Americans were barred from serving in the same units as white soldiers; gay soldiers, however, have not been barred from serving since 1994, when DADT became law and lifted the ban on their service. The only restriction on gay soldiers is that they not acknowledge their sexuality. In this way, gay soldiers can serve in the military by hiding their identity, which African Americans were unable to do. In fact, a 2010 Department of Defense survey found that nearly 70 percent of military service members said they had served in a unit with someone who was probably gay. "The fact is that homosexuals serve honorably in the military," says former marine Mackubin Thomas Owens. "That was the purpose of the 'don't ask, don't tell' policy compromise adopted by the [Bill] Clinton administration after Congress passed the current law prohibiting service by open homosexuals. As a result of this policy, homosexuals who are willing to subordinate their 'sexual orientation' to their duty are allowed for the most part to serve without interference." (Owens) Gays are already allowed to serve in the military—all DADT requires is that they, like every other enlisted person, put their identity as a soldier before any other.

> This statistic was taken from Appendix A in this book. Look for other pieces of information that can be used to support essays.

Paragraph 5

The desire to turn gays in the military into a civil rights issue is a misguided effort that misunderstands the very nature of military service. The military is unlike any other part of American society and therefore should not be subject to the same expectations. Prohibiting openly gay soldiers from serving does not violate their civil rights and is consistent with military realities.

> Note how the essay's conclusion wraps up the topic in a final, memorable way—without repeating every single point made in the essay.

Works Cited

Martin, Andy. "'Gays in the Military' Is Political Malarkey and a Massive Obamination." ContrarianCommentary.com. 19 Dec 2010. < http://contrariancommentary.wordpress.com/2010/12/19/andy-martin-"gays-in-the-military"-is-political-malarkey-and-a-massive-obamination/>. Accessed June 15, 2011.

McPeak, Merrill A. "Don't Change 'Don't Ask, Don't Tell.'" *New York Times* 4 Mar 2010: A27. < http://www.nytimes.com/2010/03/05/opinion/Q5mcpeak.html?r=1&adxnnl=1 &pagewanted=all&adxnnlx=1296154893-HqYOKk4U+p6/todDW8c1cO>. Accessed June 10, 2011.

Owens, Mackubin Thomas. "Repealing 'Don't Ask' Will Weaken the US Military." *Weekly Standard* 3 Dec 2010. < https://www.weeklystandard.com/blogs/repealing-dont-ask-will-weaken-us-military520652.html?nopager=l>. Accessed June 15, 2011.

Essay One Exercises

Exercise 1A: Create an Outline from an Existing Essay

It often helps to create an outline of the five-paragraph essay before you write it. The outline can help you organize the information, arguments, and evidence you have gathered during your research.

For this exercise, create an outline that could have been used to write "America's Confusion: Openly Gay Soldiers and Civil Rights in the Military." This "reverse engineering" exercise is meant to help familiarize you with how outlines can help classify and arrange information.

To do this you will need to
1. articulate the essay's thesis
2. pinpoint important pieces of evidence
3. flag quotes that supported the essay's ideas, and
4. identify key points that supported the argument.

Part of the outline has already been started to give you an idea of the assignment.

Outline

I. Paragraph One
Write the essay's thesis:

II. Paragraph Two
Topic: The military is not a democracy, nor should it be.

Supporting Detail i.

Supporting Detail ii. The point that military functionality depends on taking orders, obeying, and not questioning, interpreting, or veering from the plan: In other words, the very opposite of what occurs in a democracy.

III. Paragraph Three
Topic:

    i. Quote from former air force chief of staff Merrill A. McPeak.

    ii.

IV. Paragraph Four
Topic: The ban on openly gay soldiers is nothing like the ban on African American soldiers serving with whites in the early twentieth century.

    i.

    ii.

V. Paragraph Five:
Write the essay's conclusion:

Exercise 1B: Create an Outline for Your Own Essay

The model essay you just read expresses a particular point of view about gays in the military. For this exercise, your assignment is to find supporting ideas, choose specific and concrete details, create an outline, and ultimately write a five-paragraph essay making a different, or even opposing, point. Your goal is to use persuasive techniques to convince your reader.

Part I: Write a thesis statement.

The following thesis statement would be appropriate for an opposing essay on why banning openly gay people from serving in the military violates their civil rights:

Forcing gay servicemen and servicewomen to stay closeted treats them like second-class soldiers and denies them critical and much-deserved benefits.

Or, see the sample topics suggested in Appendix D for more ideas.

Part II: Brainstorm pieces of supporting evidence.

Using information from some of the viewpoints in the previous section and from the information found in Section Three of this book, write down three arguments or pieces of evidence that support the thesis statement you selected. Then, for each of these three arguments, write down supportive facts, examples, and details that support it. These could be:

- statistical information
- personal memories and anecdotes
- quotes from experts, peers, or family members
- observations of people's actions and behaviors
- specific and concrete details

Supporting pieces of evidence for the above sample thesis statement are found in this book, and include:

- Points made in Viewpoint One by Gabriel Arana about how Don't Ask, Don't Tell (DADT) encourages the harassment and assault of gay and lesbian soldiers, denies them recourse or legal protection, and institutionalizes homophobia and discrimination.
- Quote box accompanying Viewpoint Three titled "DADT Threatened Soldiers and Their Families,"

which argues that gay soldiers and their families are at risk of being blackmailed when they are forced to keep their sexuality a secret.
- Article listed in the bibliography: Daniel Redman and Ilona Turner, "Don't Ask, Don't Tell—Anyone, Anywhere," *Nation*, November 16, 2010. www.thenation.com/article/156477/dont-ask-dont-tell-anyone-anywhere. This article contains information about the kinds of benefits and activities that are denied to closeted gay soldiers and their families.
- Quote box accompanying Viewpoint One by Paul James titled "Allowing Openly Gay Soldiers to Serve Protects Their Civil Rights," which argues that DADT legalized discrimination.
- Statistics listed in Appendix A from a 2010 Quinnipiac University poll, which found that 66 percent of Americans think that preventing openly gay men and women from serving in the military is discrimination and that 43 percent of Americans think the Pentagon should provide benefits for the domestic partners of gay personnel.

Part III: Place the information from Part I in outline form.

Part IV: Write the arguments or supporting statements in paragraph form.

By now you have three arguments that support the paragraph's thesis statement, as well as supporting material. Use the outline to write out your three supporting arguments in paragraph form. Make sure each paragraph has a topic sentence that states the paragraph's thesis clearly and broadly. Then, add supporting sentences that express the facts, quotes, details, and examples that support the paragraph's thesis. The paragraph may also have a concluding or summary sentence.

Essay Two

A Gay-Friendly Military Is a Weakened Military

Editor's Notes The following model essay argues that openly gay soldiers will weaken the US military. Like the first model essay, this essay is structured as a five-paragraph persuasive essay in which each paragraph contributes a supporting piece of evidence to develop the argument. Each supporting paragraph explores one of three distinct ways in which the author thinks that openly gay soldiers will hamper the military.

As you read this essay, take note of its components and how they are organized (the sidebars in the margins provide further explanation).

- Refers to thesis and topic sentences
- Refers to supporting details

Paragraph 1

When Don't Ask, Don't Tell (DADT) was repealed in 2010, Congress cleared the way for allowing openly gay soldiers to serve in the military. Yet it did so without sufficient concern for how this policy change will threaten the military's effectiveness. Allowing openly gay soldiers will hurt the military in three main ways: It will cause a mass exodus of soldiers, impair America's reputation overseas, and weaken the bonds among soldiers in a unit. For all of these reasons, the DADT repeal should not be allowed to stand.

This is the essay's thesis statement. It tells the reader what will be argued in the following paragraph.

Paragraph 2

A primary way in which the new policy will weaken the US military is by causing the departure of thousands of highly trained and qualified soldiers who do not want to serve alongside openly gay soldiers. In fact, a 2010 study of enlisted soldiers found that huge numbers would leave the army if DADT were repealed: Just over 21 percent of army combat personnel said they would leave sooner than they had originally planned to; almost 15 percent

This is the topic sentence of Paragraph 2. It tells what piece of the argument this paragraph will focus on.

said they would consider leaving. Combined, that represents a total potential loss of more than a third of army combat troops. Among the marines, even more would leave: the survey found that 32 percent of marines said they would leave sooner than planned, and more than 16 percent would consider leaving, period. In other words, nearly half of all marines would leave or consider leaving. Warns Elaine Donnelly of the Center for Military Readiness, "The gradual loss of so many combat troops . . . could put remaining troops in greater danger, and break the All-Volunteer Force."

> *This fact helps support the paragraph's main idea: that soldiers will resign if forced to serve with openly gay troops. Get in the habit of supporting the points you make with facts, quotes, statistics, and anecdotes.*

> *Note how this quote supports the ideas discussed in the paragraph. It also comes from a reputable source.*

Paragraph 3

Letting gay and lesbian soldiers serve openly in the armed forces could also make it difficult for the United States to attract allies and might even unite enemies against us. In many nations—especially Muslim ones—homosexuality is considered a grave sin and a crime. It is likely, then, that a gay-friendly military would make some nations wary of serving alongside US soldiers; it may even give particularly religious nations cause to actively oppose us. "All major religions teach the primacy of sex between husbands and wives and the immorality of homosexuality," argues Christian writer Robert Knight. "Enforcing acceptance of homosexuality may endear us to the weak sisters of Western Europe, but it puts the United States military in conflict with universal moral traditions. Between this and Hollywood, it shouldn't be hard for our enemies to make an even stronger case that we're 'the Great Satan.'" (Knight) It doesn't take a genius to realize that once the word gets out that the U.S. military is gay-friendly, it won't be hard for fundamentalists to whip up even more anti-U.S. sentiment.

> *What is the topic sentence of Paragraph 3? How did you recognize it?*

> *What point in Paragraph 3 does this quote support?*

Paragraph 4

A third, but by no means final, way in which out-and-proud homosexuals will weaken the military is by hampering units' ability to function effectively. Military units thrive on the tight-knit relationships among soldiers.

> "Yet" is a transitional phrase that keeps the ideas flowing. See Preface B for a list of such words commonly found in persuasive essays.

> Identify a piece of evidence used to support Paragraph 4's main idea.

Yet it is essential that these relationships be platonic—sexual tension or prioritized relationships will introduce a dangerous inequality that will ruin unit cohesion. Straight soldiers will not want their gay comrades to be ogling or lusting after them, and unit equality will suffer if some soldiers become romantically involved and put their partner above others in their unit. As one columnist has put it, "Whenever sex is introduced . . . group cohesion crumbles." (Koehl)

Paragraph 5

The US military is no place to conduct social experiments. There is too much at risk and too much at stake. When considering whether to let openly gay soldiers serve in the military, we should listen to the soldiers themselves. After all, they are the ones who must live the day-to-day realities imposed by policies that come from above. They are telling us not to sacrifice unit cohesion, military readiness, and troop morale so that some soldiers can be open about their sexuality. Listen to the soldiers, and they will tell you to keep Don't Ask, Don't Tell.

Works Cited

Donnelly, Elaine. "'Don't Ask, Don't Tell' Repeal: Congress Ignores Combat Troops." Big Peace.com 19 Dec 2010. < http://bigpeace.com/edonnelly/2010/12/19/dont-ask-dont-tell-repeal-congress-ignores-combat-troops/ >. Accessed June 10, 2011.

Knight, Robert. "A New Meaning for 'Brothers in Arms.'" *Washington Times* 20 Dec 2010. < http://www.washingtontimes.com/news/2010/dec/20/a-new-meaning-for-brothers-in-arms/?page = 1 >. Accessed June 10, 2011.

Koehl, Stuart. "Don't Repeal 'Don't Ask/Don't Tell.'" *Weekly Standard* 15 June 2010. < https://www.weeklystandard.com/blogs/dont-repeal-dont-askdont-tell?nopager = 1 >. Accessed June 10, 2011.

Exercise 2A: Create an Outline from an Existing Essay

As you did for the first model essay in this section, create an outline that could have been used to write "A Gay-Friendly Military Is a Weakened Military." Be sure to identify the essay's thesis statement, its supporting ideas and details, and key pieces of evidence that were used.

Exercise 2B: Identify Persuasive Techniques

Essayists use many techniques to get you to agree with their ideas or to do something they want you to do. Some of the most common techniques were described in Preface B of this section titled "The Persuasive Essay." These tools are *facts* and *statistics*, *opinions*, *testimonials*, *examples*, *anecdotes*, *appeals to reason*, *appeals to emotion*, *ridicule* and *name-calling*, and *bandwagon*. Go back to the preface and review these tools. Remember that most of these tools can be used to enhance your essay, but some of them—particularly ridiculing, name-calling, and bandwagon—can detract from the essay's effectiveness. Nevertheless, you should be able to recognize them in the essays you read.

Some writers use one persuasive tool throughout their whole essay. For example, the essay may be one extended anecdote, or the writer may rely entirely on statistics. But most writers typically use a combination of persuasive tools. For example, Essay Two, "A Gay-Friendly Military Is a Weakened Military," does this.

Problem One
Read Essay Two again and see if you can find every persuasive tool used. Put that information in the following table. Part of the table is filled in for you. Explanatory notes are underneath the table. (NOTE: You will not fill in every box. No paragraph contains all of the techniques.)

	Paragraph 1 Sentence #	Paragraph 2 Sentence #	Paragraph 3 Sentence #	Paragraph 4 Sentence #	Paragraph 5 Sentence #
Fact					
Statistic		6a			
Opinion		8a			
Testimonial					
Example					
Anecdote					
Appeal to Reason					
Appeal to Emotion				4d	
Ridicule			7c		
Name-Calling					
Bandwagon					

Notes

a. That 32 percent of marines said they would leave the military sooner than planned if openly gay people were to serve is a *statistic*.

b. Donnelly's statement that "the gradual loss of so many combat troops . . . could put remaining troops in greater danger, and break the All-Volunteer Force" is an *opinion*.

c. The author is resorting to *ridicule* when she says, "It doesn't take a genius to realize. . . . "

d. The author is appealing to the reader's sense of *emotion* when she assures the reader that "straight soldiers will not want their gay comrades to be ogling or lusting after them. . . . "

Now, look at the table you have produced. Which persuasive tools does this essay rely on most heavily? Which are not used at all?

Problem Two
Apply this exercise to the other model essays in this section, and the viewpoints in Section One, after you have read them.

The Military's Loss

Essay Three

Editor's Notes The final model essay argues that highly skilled, badly needed soldiers are lost by not allowing gay people to serve in the military. Supported by facts, quotes, statistics, and opinions, it tries to persuade the reader that gay soldiers possess hard-to-come-by skills that the military needs as it struggles to fight two wars and manage other overseas commitments. The author concludes that the military cannot afford to lose the skills and talents of soldiers who happen to be gay or lesbian.

This essay differs from the previous model essays in that it is longer than five paragraphs. Sometimes five paragraphs are simply not enough to adequately develop an idea. Extending the length of an essay allows the reader to explore a topic in more depth or present multiple pieces of evidence that together provide a complete picture of a topic. Longer essays can also help readers discover the complexity of a subject by examining a topic beyond its superficial exterior. Moreover, the ability to write a sustained research or position paper is a valuable skill you will need as you advance academically.

As you read, consider the questions posed in the margins. Continue to identify thesis statements, supporting details, transitions, and quotations. Examine the introductory and concluding paragraphs to understand how they give shape to the essay. Finally, evaluate the essay's general structure and assess its overall effectiveness.

■ Refers to thesis and topic sentences

■ Refers to supporting details

Paragraph 1

As of 2011, almost fourteen thousand men and women had been discharged from the military under the Don't Ask, Don't Tell (DADT) policy because of their sexual orientation. These soldiers were otherwise qualified for service; they possessed skills and talents that benefited the military and the country they served. But because

What is the essay's thesis statement? How did you recognize it?

DADT (repealed in 2011) prohibits the service of lesbian, gay, and bisexual soldiers, thousands of highly trained, valuable soldiers were either asked to resign or forcibly kicked out. The loss of these highly qualified men and women should concern all Americans who expect their military to attract and retain the best people the nation has to offer.

Paragraph 2

One of the most critical groups affected by DADT has been Arabic-speaking soldiers. As of 2010, at least sixty-four linguists—language experts who are fluent in both English and Arabic—have been dismissed by the military because of their sexual orientation. One of these people was Daniel Choi. The *Times* of London reports that Choi led combat patrols in a particularly dangerous area of Iraq known as "The Triangle of Death." He also translated highly sensitive and valuable documents and other communications for the troops he worked with. Skilled also in engineering, Choi helped rebuild schools and hospitals in Iraq during his tour of duty. Despite being an officer with the rank of lieutenant, a West Point graduate, an Iraq War veteran, and a skilled linguist, Choi was ultimately kicked out of the army. "His departure will be a significant loss for the military," noted reporter Catherine Philp. (Philp)

What point do these details directly support?

Paragraph 3

Stephen Benjamin is another Arabic-language specialist who was dismissed from the military because of his sexual orientation. Benjamin notes that dismissing Arabic translators from the military is particularly short-sighted and damaging to national security. "The lack of qualified translators has been a pressing issue for some time," he notes, arguing that the US military cannot afford to lose more of them simply because they are gay. "More than 58 Arabic linguists have been kicked out since 'don't ask, don't tell' was instituted. How much valuable intelligence could those men and women be providing today to troops in harm's way?" (Benjamin)

This quote was taken from Viewpoint Six. When you see particularly striking quotes, save them to use to support points in your essays.

Paragraph 4

The same question has been asked about Sergeant Jed Anderson, who, as an Arab linguist working in Iraq, translated intelligence that was crucial to saving the lives of American troops. Anderson's job included translating and analyzing enemy communications. As he plainly puts it, "I gained information that saved American lives." (Qtd. in Suderow) Anderson eventually became the top linguist in his brigade and was honored when chosen to be a personal interpreter for a colonel. His role in the Iraq war effort was described as "crucial"—nevertheless, he was discharged for the crime of "committing 'homosexual acts.'" (Qtd. in Suderow) Interestingly, his commander realized the loss Anderson's dismissal would pose to his unit: When Anderson first submitted a formal letter acknowledging his sexuality, his commander refused to recognize it, saying, "I won't lose a good soldier to a stupid policy." (Qtd. in Suderow) Ultimately, of course, both had to comply with DADT.

> Identify a piece of evidence used to support Paragraph 4's main idea.

> Analyze this quote. What do you think made the author want to select it for inclusion in the essay?

Paragraph 5

The military also lost the skills of Anthony Loverde. Though not an Arabic translator, Loverde is highly skilled in flying and in technical operations. Loverde was kicked out of the military in 2008 after he admitted his sexuality to his commander. Loverde has argued that his loss is also the military's—two long wars have made it more difficult to recruit Americans willing to fight, and he thinks it is ridiculous that he should be turned away when he is trained and willing to fight. "Our military is stretched thin," he wrote in the *Washington Post* in 2010. "We need everyone we can get in the fight." Interestingly, the military's loss was a defense contractor's gain: Shortly after his dismissal, a private defense company hired Loverde to do basically the same job he had done for the military. He even worked as a contractor next to some of the very people with whom he had formerly served. That Loverde's skills are being tapped by a private company rather than the nation he wishes to serve is a sad reality, indeed.

> Make a list of all the transitions that appear in the essay and how they keep the ideas flowing.

Paragraph 6

In addition to active duty military, DADT has stifled and soured the careers of many promising military cadets as well. Case in point is Katherine Miller, who in 2010 resigned from the prestigious US Military Academy at West Point because she admitted to being a lesbian. The loss of Miller decidedly stings, as she was a very good student. She was ranked ninth in her class of more than eleven hundred cadets, boasted a grade point average of 3.829 out of 4.0, and scored very high on the military's fitness test, in addition to other achievements. Jim Fox, a spokesman for the military academy, described Miller as having been "in good standing and has done very well academically, militarily and physically." (Qtd in Associated Press) Miller would have gone on to graduate, join the army, and serve her country with honors, except that she could not stand the thought of living a lie during all that time. "To make a commitment of ten years, not knowing for sure that she wouldn't be hiding for the next decade, I think was just too much," said West Point graduate Sue Fulton of the group Knights Out, which opposes DADT. (Qtd. in Wetenhall)

What is the topic sentence of Paragraph 6? Look for a sentence that tells generally what the paragraph's main point is.

Paragraph 7

In addition to specific personnel losses, the military has suffered hypothetical losses, too. This was the conclusion of a March 2007 study by the Williams Institute at UCLA, which estimated that had DADT never been adopted, the military would now have thousands more soldiers in its ranks. "Since the initiation of the DADT policy in 1994," the study found, "an average of nearly 4,000 LGB [lesbian, gay, and bisexual] military personnel each year on active duty or in the guard or reserves would have been retained if they could have been more open about their sexual orientation." (Gates) Over the years, that adds up to tens of thousands of soldiers that the military lost. Add to this the countless number of Americans who have chosen not to enlist at all, and it is clear that DADT has prevented a significant number of skilled personnel from serving their country.

What is the topic sentence of Paragraph 7? How is it different but related to the other topics discussed in the essay to this point?

Paragraph 8

The loss of so many skilled soldiers clearly upsets the American public, enough so that they no longer support the policy that has kept skilled people from keeping them safe. In fact, "voters value skills over sexual orientation" was the conclusion of a 2010 Center for American Progress survey that found that 60 percent of Americans said that with the United States bogged down in wars in both Iraq and Afghanistan, "the military needs every talented woman and man it can get regardless of a person's sexual orientation." (Krehely and Teixeira) The American public has loudly stated it wants its military to be composed of the most talented and skilled soldiers possible, regardless of their sexual orientation.

> What pieces of this essay are opinions? What parts are facts? Make a list of opinions and facts and see which the author relies on more.

Paragraph 9

"I'm trained to fight, I speak Arabic, and I'm willing to serve." These were the words of Stephen Benjamin as he declared, even after his humiliating dismissal, his continuing desire to use his highly coveted skills to serve his country. The United States must make sure that something as inconsequential as sexual orientation does not prevent people like Benjamin from serving their country and protecting their fellow Americans.

> After reading the essay, are you convinced of the author's point? If so, what evidence swayed you? If not, why not?

Works Cited

Associated Press. "Lesbian Cadet Quits West Point, Cites 'Don't Ask.'" *Seattle Times* 12 Aug 2010. < http://seattletimes.nwsource.com/html/nationworld/2012605545_apuswestpointlesbiancadet.html >. Accessed June 9, 2011.

Benjamin, Stephen. "Don't Ask, Don't Translate." *New York Times* 8 June 2007. < http://www.nytimes.com/2007/06/08/opinion/08benjamin.html >. Accessed June 9, 2011.

Gates, Gary J. "Effects of 'Don't Ask, Don't Tell' on Retention Among Lesbian, Gay, and Bisexual Military

Personnel." Williams Institute, University of California, Los Angeles, School of Law March 2007. <http://www3.law.ucla.edu/williamsinstitute/publications/EffectsOfDontAskDontTellOnRetention.pdf>. Accessed June 9, 2011

Krehely, Jeff, and Ruy Teixeira. "Americans Support Repeal of "Don't Ask Don't Tell." Center for American Progress 17 Feb 2010. <http://www.americanprogress.org/issues/2010/02/dadt_poll.html>. Accessed June 9, 2011.

Loverde, Anthony. "'Don't Ask, Don't Tell' Ended My Military Career, but Not My Service." *Washington Post* 5 Feb 2010. <http://www.washingtonpost.com/wp-dyn/content/article/2010/02/05/AR2010020501444.html>. Accessed June 9, 2011.

Philp, Catherine. "Dan Choi Ordered Out of US Military for Announcing His Homosexuality." *Times* (London) 2 July 2009. <http://www.timesonline.co.uk/tol/news/world/us_and_americas/article6620287.ece>. Accessed June 9, 2011.

Suderow, Sasha. "Don't Ask Don't Tell: A Story Highlighting the Anguish Faced by Soldiers with Indispensable Skills." *Huffington Post* 12 Mar 2010. <http://www.huffingtonpost.com/sasha-suderow/dont-ask-dont-tell-a-Stor_b 496565.html>. Accessed June 9, 2011.

Wetenhall, John. "Top Ranked Lesbian Cadet Leaves West Point." ABC News. 13 Aug 2010. <http://abcnews.go.com/US/lesbian-west-point-cadet-resigns/story?id=11395858>. Accessed June 9, 2011.

Exercise 3A: Examining Introductions and Conclusions

Every essay features introductory and concluding paragraphs that are used to frame the main ideas being presented. Along with presenting the essay's thesis statement, well-written introductions should grab the attention of the reader and make clear why the topic being explored is important. The conclusion reiterates the essay's thesis and is also the last chance for the writer to make an impression on the reader. Strong introductions and conclusions can greatly enhance an essay's effect on an audience.

The Introduction

There are several techniques that can be used to craft an introductory paragraph. An essay can start with:

- an anecdote: a brief story that illustrates a point relevant to the topic;
- startling information: facts or statistics that elucidate the point of the essay;
- setting up and knocking down a position: a position or claim believed by proponents of one side of a controversy, followed by statements that challenge that claim;
- historical perspective: an example of the way things used to be that leads into a discussion of how or why things work differently now;
- summary information: general introductory information about the topic that feeds into the essay's thesis statement.

Problem One
Reread the introductory paragraphs of the model essays and of the viewpoints in Section One. Identify which of the techniques described above are used in the example essays. How do they grab the attention of the reader? Are their thesis statements clearly presented?

Problem Two
Write an introduction for the essay you have outlined and partially written in Exercise 1B using one of the techniques described above.

The Conclusion

The conclusion brings the essay to a close by summarizing or returning to its main ideas. Good conclusions, however, go beyond simply repeating these ideas. Strong conclusions explore a topic's broader implications and reiterate why it is important to consider. They may frame the essay by returning to an anecdote featured in the opening paragraph. Or, they may close with a quotation or refer back to an event in the essay. In opinionated essays, the conclusion can reiterate which side the essay is taking or ask the reader to reconsider a previously held position on the subject.

Problem Three
Reread the concluding paragraphs of the model essays and of the viewpoints in Section One. Which were most effective in driving their arguments home to the reader? What sorts of techniques did they use to do this? Did they appeal emotionally to the reader, or bookend an idea or event referenced elsewhere in the essay?

Problem Four
Write a conclusion for the essay you have outlined and partially written in Exercise 1B using one of the techniques described above.

Exercise 3B: Using Quotations to Enliven Your Essay

No essay is complete without quotations. Get in the habit of using quotes to support at least some of the ideas in your essays. Quotes do not need to appear in every paragraph, but often enough so that the essay contains voices besides your own. When you write, use quotations to accomplish the following:

- Provide expert advice that you are not necessarily in the position to know about
- Cite lively or passionate passages
- Include a particularly well-written point that gets to the heart of the matter
- Supply statistics or facts that have been derived from someone's research
- Deliver anecdotes that illustrate the point you are trying to make
- Express first-person testimony

Problem One
Reread the essays presented in all sections of this book and find at least one example of each of the above quotation types.

There are a couple of important things to remember when using quotations.

- Note your sources' qualifications and biases. This way your reader can identify the person you have quoted and can put their words in a context.
- Put any quoted material within proper quotation marks. Failing to attribute quotes to their authors constitutes plagiarism, which is when an author takes someone else's words or ideas and presents them as his or her own. Plagiarism is a very serious matter and must be avoided at all costs.

Final Writing Challenge

Write Your Own Persuasive Five-Paragraph Essay

Using the information from this book, write your own five-paragraph persuasive essay that deals with gays in the military. You can use the resources in this book for information about issues relating to this topic and how to structure this type of essay.

The following steps are suggestions on how to get started.

Step One: Choose your topic.
The first step is to decide what topic to write your persuasive essay on. Is there anything that particularly fascinates you about gays in the military or Don't Ask, Don't Tell? Is there an aspect of the topic you strongly support or feel strongly against? Is there an issue you feel personally connected to or one that you would like to learn more about? Ask yourself such questions before selecting your essay topic. Refer to Appendix D: Sample Essay Topics if you need help selecting a topic.

Step Two: Write down questions and answers about the topic.
Before you begin writing, you will need to think carefully about what ideas your essay will contain. This is a process known as *brainstorming*. Brainstorming involves asking yourself questions and coming up with ideas to discuss in your essay. Possible questions that will help you with the brainstorming process include:
- Why is this topic important?
- Why should people be interested in this topic?
- How can I make this essay interesting to the reader?
- What question am I going to address in this paragraph or essay?
- What facts, ideas, or quotes can I use to support the answer to my question?

Questions especially suited to persuasive essays include:
- Is there something I want to convince my reader of?
- Is there a topic I want to advocate for or rally people against?

86

- Is there enough evidence to support my opinion?
- Do I want to make a call to action; that is, motivate my readers to do something about a particular problem or event?

Step Three: Gather facts, ideas, and anecdotes related to your topic.
This book contains several places to find information about many aspects of military service and sexual orientation, including the viewpoints and the appendices. In addition, you may want to research the books, articles, and websites listed in Section Three or do additional research in your local library. You can also conduct interviews if you know someone who has a compelling story that would fit well in your essay.

Step Four: Develop a workable thesis statement.
Use what you have written down in steps two and three to help you articulate the main point or argument you want to make in your essay. It should be expressed in a clear sentence and make an arguable or supportable point.

Example:
Gays should be prevented from serving openly in the military for their own protection.
(This could be the thesis statement of a persuasive essay that argues against repealing Don't Ask, Don't Tell on the grounds that openly gay servicemen and servicewomen would be threatened, mocked, physically assaulted, or even killed by intolerant, homophobic soldiers.)

Step Five: Write an outline or diagram.
a. Write the thesis statement at the top of the outline.
b. Write roman numerals I, II, and III on the left side of the page. Under each numeral write the letters A, B, and C.
c. Next to each roman numeral, write down the best ideas you came up with in step three. These should all directly relate to and support the thesis statement.
d. Next to each letter write down information that supports that particular idea.

Step Six: Write the three supporting paragraphs.
Use your outline to write the three supporting paragraphs. Write down the main idea of each paragraph in sentence form. Do the same thing for the supporting points of information. Each sentence should support the topic of the paragraph. Be sure you have relevant and interesting details, facts, and quotes. Use transitional words and phrases when you move from idea to idea to keep the text fluid and smooth. Sometimes, although not always, paragraphs can include a concluding or summary sentence that restates the paragraph's argument.

Step Seven: Write the introduction and conclusion.
See Exercise 3A for information on writing introductions and conclusions.

Step Eight: Read and rewrite.
As you read, check your essay for the following:

- ✔ Does the essay maintain a consistent tone?
- ✔ Do all paragraphs reinforce your general thesis?
- ✔ Do all paragraphs flow from one to the other? Do you need to add transitional words or phrases?
- ✔ Have you quoted from reliable, authoritative, and interesting sources?
- ✔ Is there a sense of progression throughout the essay?
- ✔ Does the essay get bogged down in too much detail or irrelevant material?
- ✔ Does your introduction grab the reader's attention?
- ✔ Does your conclusion reflect back on any previously discussed material or give the essay a sense of closure?
- ✔ Are there any spelling or grammatical errors?

Section Three: Supporting Research Material

Appendix A

Facts About Gays in the Military

Editor's Note: These facts can be used in reports to add credibility when making important arguments.

Facts About Don't Ask, Don't Tell (DADT)

DADT became official US policy when President Bill Clinton signed the 1994 National Defense Authorization Act.

It prohibited soldiers from admitting to homosexual acts or lifestyle and from being asked about their sexuality on military applications.

The Supreme Court upheld the constitutionality of DADT in the 1998 case *Andrew Holmes v. California Army National Guard*.

Congress voted to repeal DADT in December 2010.

The repeal was implemented on September 20, 2011, after the Pentagon declared that repealing DADT would not undermine the military's effectiveness or its recruiting.

According to data from the Department of Defense, the Department of Homeland Security, and the Army National Guard Bureau:
- 14,055 soldiers were discharged because of their sexual orientation between 1994 and 2009;
- the most soldiers were discharged in 2001 (1,273);
- the fewest soldiers were discharged in 2009 (428); and
- in 2009, about 80 percent of those discharged came forward themselves and acknowledged that they were gay while about 20 percent were outed to superiors against their will by a third party.

A study by the Williams Institute at UCLA School of Law found that repealing DADT could increase military ranks by more than thirty-six thousand members.

According to Williams Institute researchers, implementing DADT cost the military between $290 million and more than $500 million since its inception in 1994. The military spent an estimated $22,000 to $43,000 per person to replace those discharged under DADT.

A 2010 report by the conservative Family Research Council found that 8.2 percent of all military sexual assault cases were homosexual in nature.

The Family Research Council estimates that just 1.26 percent of military personnel are gay men, and just 0.97 percent are lesbian.

Gay Soldiers and Military Service Around the World

In May 2010 the *Christian Science Monitor* reported that the United States and Turkey were the only NATO (North Atlantic Treaty Organization, a defense alliance) members to *not* allow gays and lesbians to openly serve in the military.

According to the University of California Santa Barbara's Palm Center:
- Besides the United States, at least twenty-five countries specifically allow gays and lesbians to serve in the military. These include Austria, Belgium, Canada, the Czech Republic, Denmark, Estonia, Finland, France, Germany, Ireland, Israel, Italy, Lithuania, Luxembourg, the Netherlands, New Zealand, Norway, Slovenia, South Africa, Spain, Sweden, Switzerland, Taiwan, the United Kingdom, and Uruguay.

- Sixteen countries—including Pakistan, Syria, Venezuela, and Yemen—bar open homosexuals from serving in the military.
- Homosexuality is illegal in thirty-seven African nations, both in the military and in society in general.

Military Opinions About Gays in the Military

A comprehensive survey conducted by the Department of Defense in 2010 solicited the views of over a hundred thousand active duty and reserve service members. It found the following about troops' opinions on the Don't Ask, Don't Tell policy and the possibility of openly gay soldiers serving in the military.

Troops were asked how working with an openly gay or lesbian service member would affect various aspects of their jobs. The results showed that
- 18.4 percent said it would positively/very positively affect their unit's ability to work together to get the job done;
- 32.1 percent said it would equally positively and negatively affect their unit's ability to work together to get the job done;
- 26.9 percent said it would negatively/very negatively affect their unit's ability to work together to get the job done;
- 19.9 percent said it would have no effect;

- 18.1 percent said it would positively/very positively affect their unit's ability to trust each other;
- 31.2 percent said it would equally positively and negatively affect their unit's ability to trust each other;
- 33.1 percent said it would negatively/very negatively affect their unit's ability to trust each other;
- 17.6 percent said it would have no effect;

- 18.1 percent said it would positively/very positively affect their unit's ability to care for each other;
- 33.6 percent said it would equally positively and negatively affect their unit's ability to care for each other;
- 30.0 percent said it would negatively/very negatively affect their unit's ability to care for each other;
- 18.4 percent said it would have no effect.

When service members with combat experience were asked how working with an openly gay soldier would affect their immediate unit's effectiveness in completing its mission in an intense combat situation, the response was:
- 12.4 percent said positively/very positively;
- 31.4 percent said equally positively and negatively;
- 25.6 percent said no effect;
- 30.6 percent said negatively/very negatively.

When service members with combat experience were asked how working with an openly gay soldier would affect their immediate unit's effectiveness at completing its mission in a field environment or out to sea, the response was:
- 11.4 percent said positively/very positively;
- 25.8 percent said equally positively and negatively;
- 18.6 percent said no effect;
- 44.3 percent said negatively/very negatively.

When service members were asked what they would most likely do in the event they were assigned to bathroom facilities with an open-bay shower that was also used by gay soldiers who were allowed to be openly gay, the response was:
- 29.4 percent said they would take no action;
- 25.8 percent said they would use the shower at a different time;
- 11.0 percent said they would discuss with that person how they expect each other to behave and conduct themselves;

- 1.3 percent said they would talk to a chaplain or leader about how to handle the situation;
- 17.7 percent said they would talk to a leader to see if they had other options;
- 7.0 percent said they would do something else;
- 7.9 percent said they did not know.

When service members were asked what they would most likely do in the event they had to share a room, berth, or field tent with someone that was allowed to be openly gay, the reponse was:
- 26.7 percent said they would take no action;
- 24.2 percent said they would discuss with that person how they expect each other to behave and conduct themselves while sharing a room, berth, or field tent;
- 2.4 percent said they would talk to a chaplain, mentor, or leader about how to handle the situation;
- 28.1 percent said they would talk to a leader to see if they have other options;
- 8.7 percent said they would do something else;
- 9.9 percent said they did not know.

Service members were also asked the following questions prior to the repeal of DADT:

How would the repeal of DADT affect your personal readiness?
- 7.1 percent said the repeal of DADT would positively/very positively affect their personal readiness;
- 60.0 percent said it would equally positively and negatively affect their personal readiness;
- 11.5 percent said it would negatively/very negatively affect their personal readiness;
- 21.5 percent said it would have no effect on their personal readiness.

How would the repeal of DADT affect your ability to train well?
- 7.3 percent said it would positively/very positively affect their ability to train well;

- 51.1 percent said it would equally positively and negatively affect their ability to train well;
- 20.8 percent said it would negatively/very negatively affect their ability to train well;
- 20.8 percent said it would have no effect.

How would the repeal of DADT affect your immediate unit's readiness?
- 6.8 percent said positively/very positively;
- 46.1 percent said equally positively and negatively;
- 21.2 percent said negatively/very negatively;
- 25.8 percent said no effect.

How would the repeal of DADT affect your unit's ability to train well together?
- 7.0 percent said positively/very positively;
- 37.1 percent said equally positively and negatively;
- 31.3 percent said negatively/very negatively;
- 24.5 percent said no effect.

If DADT is repealed, how, if at all, will your military career plans be affected?
- 62.3 percent said "my military career plans will not change";
- 1.7 percent said "I will stay longer than I had planned";
- 1.8 percent said "I will think about staying longer than I had planned";
- 11.1 percent said "I will think about leaving sooner than I had planned";
- 12.6 percent said "I will leave sooner than I had planned";
- 10.5 percent said they did not know.

How would the repeal of DADT affect your level of morale?
- 4.8 percent said positively/very positively;
- 13.2 percent said equally positively and negatively;

- 27.9 percent said negatively/very negatively;
- 43.6 percent said no effect;
- 10.5 percent said they did not know.

In your career, have you ever worked in a unit with a coworker you believed to be homosexual?
- 69.3 percent said yes;
- 30.7 percent said no.

Do you currently serve with a male or female service member you believe to be homosexual?
- 36 percent said yes;
- 64 percent said no.

Civilian Opinions About Gays in the Military

According to a December 2010 Pew Research Center survey:
- 21 percent of Americans strongly favored allowing gays and lesbians to serve openly in the military;
- 38 percent favored;
- 16 percent opposed;
- 8 percent strongly opposed;
- 17 were unsure or refused to answer.

According to a November 2010 *USA Today*/Gallup poll:
- 32 percent of Americans thought it was very important to pass legislation to allow openly gay men and women to serve in the military;
- 24 percent thought it was somewhat important;
- 18 percent thought it was not too important;
- 23 percent thought it was not at all important;
- 2 percent were unsure.

A November 2010 CNN/Opinion Research Corporation poll found that
- 72 percent of Americans said they favor permitting people who are openly gay or lesbian to serve in the military;

- 23 percent opposed;
- 5 percent were unsure.

A 2010 Quinnipiac University poll found the following about American opinions of gays in the military:
- 66 percent of Americans thought that preventing openly gay men and women from serving in the military was discrimination;
- 31 percent thought it was not;
- 3 percent were unsure.

- 30 percent of Americans thought that allowing openly gay men and women to serve in the military would be divisive for the troops and hurt their ability to fight effectively;
- 65 percent disagreed;
- 5 percent were unsure.

- 10 percent of Americans thought the military should aggressively pursue disciplinary action against gay service members whose orientation was revealed against their will by third parties;
- 82 percent favored ending this practice;
- 8 percent were unsure;

- 54 percent thought that gay military personnel should face restrictions on exhibiting their sexual orientation on the job;
- 38 percent thought they should not;
- 8 percent were unsure;
- 43 percent of Americans thought the Pentagon should be responsible for providing benefits for the domestic partners of gay personnel;
- 50 percent did not;
- 45 percent of Americans thought heterosexual military personnel should be required to share quarters with gay personnel;
- 46 percent disagreed.

Appendix B

Finding and Using Sources of Information

No matter what type of essay you are writing, it is necessary to find information to support your point of view. You can use sources such as books, magazine articles, newspaper articles, and online articles.

Using Books and Articles

You can find books and articles in a library by using the library's computer or cataloging system. If you are not sure how to use these resources, ask a librarian to help you. You can also use a computer to find many magazine articles and other articles written specifically for the Internet.

You are likely to find a lot more information than you can possibly use in your essay, so your first task is to narrow it down to what is likely to be most usable. Look at book and article titles. Look at book chapter titles, and examine the book's index to see if it contains information on the specific topic you want to write about. (For example, if you want to write about the passage of Don't Ask, Don't Tell (DADT) and you find a book about military history, check the chapter titles and index to be sure it contains information about DADT before you bother to check out the book.)

For a five-paragraph essay, you do not need a great deal of supporting information, so quickly try to narrow down your materials to a few good books and magazine or Internet articles. You do not need dozens. You might even find that one or two good books or articles contain all the information you need.

You probably do not have time to read an entire book, so find the chapters or sections that relate to your topic, and skim these. When you find useful information, copy it onto a note card or notebook. You should look for supporting facts, statistics, quotations, and examples.

Using the Internet

When you select your supporting information, it is important that you evaluate its source. This is especially important with information you find on the Internet. Because nearly anyone can put information on the Internet, there is as much bad information as good information. Before using Internet information—or any information—try to determine if the source seems to be reliable. Is the author or Internet site sponsored by a legitimate organization? Is it from a government source? Does the author have any special knowledge or training relating to the topic you are looking up? Does the article give any indication of where its information comes from?

Using Your Supporting Information

When you use supporting information from a book, article, interview, or other source, there are three important things to remember:

1. *Make it clear whether you are using a direct quotation or a paraphrase.* If you copy information directly from your source, you are quoting it. You must put quotation marks around the information, and tell where the information comes from. If you put the information in your own words, you are paraphrasing it.

2. *Use the information fairly.* Be careful to use supporting information in the way the author intended it. For example, it is unfair to quote an author as saying, "In a democracy, everyone should have the same rights" when he or she intended to say, "In a democracy, everyone should have the same rights—except that militaries are distinctly undemocratic, and for good reason." This is called taking information out of context. This is using supporting evidence unfairly.

3. *Give credit where credit is due.* Giving credit is known as citing. You must use citations when you use someone else's information, but not every piece of supporting information needs a citation.

- If the supporting information is general knowledge—that is, it can be found in many sources—you do not have to cite your source.
- If you directly quote a source, you must cite it.
- If you paraphrase information from a specific source, you must cite it.

If you do not use citations where you should, you are *plagiarizing*—or stealing—someone else's work.

Citing Your Sources

There are a number of ways to cite your sources. Your teacher will probably want you to do it in one of three ways:

- Informal: As in the example in many of the model essays presented in Section Two of this book, tell where you got the information as you present it in the text of your essay.
- Informal list: At the end of your essay, place an unnumbered list of all the sources you used. This tells the reader where, in general, your information came from.
- Formal: Use numbered footnotes or endnotes. Footnotes or endnotes are generally placed at the end of an article or essay, although they may be placed elsewhere depending on your teacher's requirements.

Appendix C

Using MLA Style to Create a Works Cited List

You will probably need to create a list of works cited for your paper. These include materials that you quoted from, relied heavily on, or consulted to write your paper. There are several different ways to structure these references. The following examples are based on Modern Language Association (MLA) style, one of the major citation styles used by writers.

Book Entries

For most book entries you will need the author's name, the book's title, where it was published, what company published it, and the year it was published. This information is usually found on the inside of the book. Variations on book entries include the following:

A book by a single author:
> Jacobs, Thomas A. *Teen Cyberbullying Investigated: Where Do Your Rights End and Consequences Begin?* Minneapolis: Free Spirit, 2010.

Two or more books by the same author:
> Pollan, Michael. *In Defense of Food: An Eater's Manifesto.* New York: Penguin, 2009.
> ———. *The Omnivore's Dilemma.* New York: Penguin, 2006.

A book by two or more authors:
> McNerney, Jerry, and Martin Cheek. *Clean Energy Nation: Freeing America from the Tyranny of Fossil Fuels.* New York: AMACOM, 2011.

A book with an editor:
>Friedman, Lauri S., ed. *Introducing Issues with Opposing Viewpoints: Torture*. Detroit: Greenhaven, 2011.

Periodical and Newspaper Entries

Entries for sources found in periodicals and newspapers are cited a bit differently than books. For one, these sources usually have a title and a publication name. They also may have specific dates and page numbers. Unlike book entries, you do not need to list where newspapers or periodicals are published or what company publishes them.

An article from a periodical:
>Burns, William C.G. "Ocean Acidification: A Greater Threat than Global Warming and Overfishing?," *Terrain* Winter/Spring 2008:169–83.

An unsigned article from a periodical:
>"Chinese Disease? The Rapid Spread of Syphilis in China." *Global Agenda* 14 Jan. 2007.

An article from a newspaper:
>Weiss, Rick. "Can Food from Cloned Animals Be Called Organic?," *Washington Post* 29 Jan. 2008: A06.

Internet Sources

To document a source you found online, try to provide as much information on it as possible, including the author's name, the title of the document, date of publication or of last revision, the URL, and your date of access.

A web source:
> De Seno, Tommy. *"Roe vs. Wade* and the Rights of the Father." Fox Forum.com 22 Jan. 2009. <http://foxforum.blogs.foxnews.com/2009/01/22/deseno_roe_wade/> Accessed May 20, 2009.

Your teacher will tell you exactly how information should be cited in your essay. Generally, the very least information needed is the original author's name and the name of the article or other publication.

Be sure you know exactly what information your teacher requires before you start looking for your supporting information so that you know what information to include with your notes.

Appendix D

Sample Essay Topics on Gays in the Military

Gay Soldiers Should Be Allowed to Serve Openly

Gay Soldiers Should Not Be Allowed to Serve Openly

Openly Gay Soldiers Should Be Restricted to Noncombat Positions

Openly Gay Soldiers Should Not Be Banned from Any Military Post or Position

Openly Gay Soldiers Will Weaken the US Military

Openly Gay Soldiers Will Strengthen the US Military

Openly Gay Soldiers Threaten Military Readiness

Openly Gay Soldiers Do Not Threaten Military Readiness

Openly Gay Soldiers Will Inspire Anti-Americanism

Openly Gay Soldiers Will Align the United States with Many of Its Allies

Openly Gay Soldiers Threaten Unit Cohesion

Openly Gay Soldiers Have No Effect on Unit Cohesion

Openly Gay Soldiers Risk Being Attacked by Fellow Troops

Military Personnel Are Not Likely to Attack Openly Gay Soldiers

Prohibiting the Service of Openly Gay Soldiers Violated Their Civil Rights

Banning Openly Gay Soldiers from Service Was Not a Civil Rights Issue

Gay Soldiers Should Not Put Their Sexuality Before Their Service

Gay Soldiers Simply Want to Live Honest, Open Lives Like Any Other Soldier

- Repealing Don't Ask, Don't Tell Was the Right Thing to Do
- Don't Ask, Don't Tell Should Not Have Been Repealed
- The Certification of The Repeal of Don't Ask, Don't Tell Was Justified
- The Repeal of Don't Ask, Don't Tell Should Not Have Been Certified
- Repealing Don't Ask, Don't Tell Was Too Expensive
- Retaining Don't Ask, Don't Tell Was Too Costly
- Attempts to Repeal DADT Reflected a Gay Political Agenda
- Attempts to Repeal DADT Reflected a Desire for Equality and Justice

Organizations to Contact

The editor has compiled the following list of organizations concerned with the issues debated in this book. The descriptions are derived from materials provided by the organizations. All have publications or information available for interested readers. The list was compiled on the date of publication of the present volume; the information provided here may change. Be aware that many organizations take several weeks or longer to respond to queries, so allow as much time as possible.

American Civil Liberties Union (ACLU)
132 W. Forty-Third St. New York, NY 10036
(212) 944-9800 • fax: (212) 359-5290
website: www.aclu.org

The ACLU is the nation's oldest and largest civil liberties organization. Its Lesbian and Gay Rights/AIDS Project, started in 1986, handles litigation, education, and public policy work on behalf of gays and lesbians and supported the repeal of Don't Ask, Don't Tell (DADT).

Center for Military Readiness (CMR)
PO Box 51600, Livonia, MI 48151
(202) 347-5333
e-mail: info@cmrlink.org • website: www.cmrlink.org

CMR is an alliance of civilian, active duty, and retired-military Americans. It is the only organization that concentrates full-time on military personnel issues. CMR's stated mission is to promote sound military personnel policies in the armed forces. It opposed the repeal of DADT, claiming that allowing gays to serve openly in the military would weaken fighting forces, threaten unit cohesion, and reduce soldiers to research subjects in an unreliable and unfair social experiment.

Concerned Women for America (CWFA)
1015 Fifteenth St. NW, Ste. 1100, Washington, DC 20005
(202) 488-7000 • fax: (202) 488-0806
e-mail: mail@cwfa.org • website: www.cwfa.org

The CWFA is an educational and legal defense foundation that seeks to strengthen the traditional family by promoting Judeo-Christian moral standards. It opposed the repeal of DADT and the granting of additional civil rights protections to gays and lesbians. The CWFA publishes the monthly magazine *Family Voice* and various position papers on gays in the military and other issues.

Family Research Council (FRC)
801 G St. NW, Washington, DC 20001
(800) 225-4008 • website: www.frc.org

The council is a research, resource, and educational organization that promotes the traditional family, which it defines as a group of people bound by marriage, blood, or adoption. It opposes marriage and adoption rights for same-sex couples and publishes numerous reports from a conservative perspective on issues affecting the family, including homosexuality and same-sex marriage. It also opposed the repeal of DADT, claiming it would weaken the US military.

Family Research Institute (FRI)
PO Box 62640, Colorado Springs, CO 80962-0640
(303) 681-3113
website: www.familyresearchinst.org

The FRI distributes information about family, sexuality, and substance abuse issues. It believes that allowing gays and lesbians to serve openly in the military undermines unit cohesion and threatens the quality of the US military. The institute publishes the bimonthly newsletter *Family Research Report* as well as numerous position papers and opinion articles.

Gay and Lesbian Advocates and Defenders (GLAD)
30 Winter St., Ste. 800, Boston, MA 02108
(617) 426-1350 • website: www.glad.org

GLAD is New England's leading legal rights organization. It is dedicated to ending discrimination based on sexual orientation, HIV status, and gender identity and expression. GLAD supported the repeal of DADT and works to support the civil rights of gay and lesbian soldiers and civilians.

Lambda Legal Defense and Education Fund, Inc.
666 Broadway, Ste. 1200, New York, NY 10012
(212) 995-8585 • website: www.lambdalegal.org

Lambda is a public-interest law firm committed to achieving full recognition of the civil rights of homosexual persons. The fund addresses a variety of areas, including equal marriage rights, the military, parenting and relationship issues, and domestic-partner benefits. It publishes the quarterly *Lambda Update* and the pamphlet *Freedom to Marry*.

National Center for Lesbian Rights
870 Market St., Ste. 570, San Francisco, CA 94102
(415) 392-6257 • website: www.nclrights.org

The center is a public-interest law office that provides legal counseling and representation for victims of sexual-orientation discrimination. Primary areas of advice include child custody and parenting, employment, housing, the military, and insurance. The group's website has a section devoted to rights for lesbian soldiers and a useful "case docket" feature that keeps tabs on court-case outcomes related to gay and lesbian rights.

Servicemembers Legal Defense Network (SLDN)
PO Box 65301, Washington DC 20035-5301
(202) 328-FAIR (328-3247) • fax: (202) 797-1635
e-mail: sldn@sldn.org • website: www.sldn.org

SLDN is a nonprofit legal-services watchdog and policy organization dedicated to ending discrimination against and harassment of military personnel affected by DADT. It worked to end DADT, ensures parity for lesbian, gay, bisexual, and transgendered (LGBT) service members, and provides free confidential legal services to all those impacted by DADT and related discrimination. Since 1993 SLDN's in-house legal team has responded to more than ten thousand requests for assistance.

Traditional Values Coalition

139 C St. SE, Washington, DC 20003
(202) 547-8570 • website: www.traditionalvalues.org

The coalition strives to restore what the group believes are traditional moral and spiritual values in American government, schools, media, and the fiber of American society. It believes that gay rights threaten the family unit and extend civil rights beyond what the coalition considers appropriate limits. The coalition publishes the quarterly newsletter *Traditional Values Report,* as well as various information papers, several of which specifically address the issue of gays in the military.

Bibliography

Books

Estes, Steve, *Ask and Tell: Gay and Lesbian Veterans Speak Out*. Chapel Hill: University of North Carolina Press, 2008. Draws on more than fifty interviews with gay and lesbian veterans to trace the evolution and history of the military's policy on homosexuality over a sixty-five-year period.

Frank, Nathaniel, *Unfriendly Fire: How the Gay Ban Undermines the Military and Weakens America*. New York: Thomas Dunne Books, 2009. Argues that the ban on openly gay and lesbian members of the US military has greatly increased discharges, hampered recruitment, and lowered morale and cohesion within military ranks.

McGowan, Jeffrey, *Major Conflict: One Gay Man's Life in the Don't-Ask-Don't-Tell Military*. New York: Broadway, 2005. A Desert Storm veteran looks back on the years he spent as a closeted soldier.

Mucciaroni, Gary, *Same Sex, Different Politics: Success and Failure in the Struggles over Gay Rights*. Chicago: University of Chicago Press, 2008. Explains why gay rights advocates have achieved dramatically different levels of success from one policy area to another. Explores debates over laws governing military service, homosexual conduct, adoption, marriage and partner recognition, hate crimes, and civil rights.

Internet Sources

Anonymous, "Confessions of a Gay Soldier," *New Republic*, September 16, 2010. www.tnr.com/article/politics/77682/confessions-gay-soldier?page = 0.0.

Barry, John, "DADT: Now the Really Hard Part Begins," *Newsweek*, December 19, 2010. www.newsweek

.com/2010/12/19/dadt-repeal-begins-a-long-tortured-process.html.

Brannon, Tom, "What a Gay Marine Taught Me," *Los Angeles Times*, December 25, 2010. http://articles.latimes.com/2010/dec/25/opinion/la-oe-brannon-dadt-20101225.

Bumiller, Elisabeth, "A How-to Guide for a New Military," *New York Times*, December 20, 2010. www.nytimes.com/2010/12/20/us/politics/20military.html?_r = 1.

Carlin, David, "Will Gays, Who Hurt Priesthood, Now Weaken Military?," *Providence (RI) Journal*, April 10, 2010. www.projo.com/opinion/contributors/content/CT_carlin10_04-10-10_FVI1D33_v7.4055788.html.

Cohen, Richard, "Someone to Lead the Marines Out of 'Don't Ask, Don't Tell,'" *Washington Post*, November 12, 2010. http://voices.washingtonpost.com/postpartisan/2010/11/dont_ask_dont_tell_and_the_mar.html.

Concerned Women for America, "Homosexuality and the Military: What 'Don't Ask, Don't Tell' Is and Why It Matters," May 19, 2010. www.cwfa.org/content.asp?id = 18936.

Donnelly, Elaine, "'Don't Ask, Don't Tell' Repeal: Congress Ignores Combat Troops," Big Peace.com, December 19, 2010. http://bigpeace.com/edonnelly/2010/12/19/dont-ask-dont-tell-repeal-congress-ignores-combat-troops/.

Espero, Will, "Homosexuality Should Not Impact Military Service," *Hawaii Reporter*, January 10, 2011. www.hawaiireporter.com/homosexuality-should-not-impact-military-service.

Fischer, Bryan, "Lame Ducks Try to Fatally Weaken US Military," RenewAmerica.com, November 25, 2010. www.renewamerica.com/columns/fischer/101125.

Harvey, Linda, "Find Sodomy Repulsive? Don't Ask, Don't Tell," World Net Daily.com, December 22, 2010. www.wnd.com/?pageId = 242521.

Herring, Elizabeth, "The Cost of DADT Repeal," *American Thinker*, December 23, 2010. www.americanthinker.com/2010/12/the_cost_of_dadt_repeal.html.

Hochstadt, Steve, "'Don't Ask, Don't Tell' Finally Becomes 'Don't Discriminate,'" *Jacksonville (IL) Journal Courier*, January 11, 2011. www.myjournalcourier.com/articles/don-31074-discriminate-homosexuality.html.

Jackson, Kevin, "The Art of War and DADT," *American Thinker*, December 23, 2010. www.americanthinker.com/2010/12/the_art_of_war_and_dadt.html.

James, Paul, "Let Open Bias Follow 'Don't Ask, Don't Tell' into Dustbin of History," *Palm Beach (FL) Post*, December 22, 2010. www.palmbeachpost.com/opinion/commentary/commentary-let-open-bias-follow-dont-ask-dont-1140709.html.

Knight, Robert, "A New Meaning for 'Brothers in Arms,'" *Washington Times*, December 20, 2010. www.washingtontimes.com/news/2010/dec/20/a-new-meaning-for-brothers-in-arms/?page=1.

Krehely, Jeff, and Ruy Teixeira, "Americans Support Repeal of 'Don't Ask Don't Tell,'" Center for American Progress, February 17, 2010. www.americanprogress.org/issues/2010/02/dadt_poll.html.

Loverde, Anthony, "'Don't Ask, Don't Tell' Ended My Military Career, but Not My Service," *Washington Post*, February 5, 2010. www.washingtonpost.com/wp-dyn/content/article/2010/02/05/AR2010020501444.html.

McPeak, Merrill A., "Don't Change 'Don't Ask, Don't Tell,'" NYTimes.com, March 4, 2010. www.nytimes.com/2010/03/05/opinion/05mcpeak.html?_r=1&adxnnl=1& pagewanted=all&adxnnlx=1296154893-HqYOKk4U+p6/todDW8clcO.

Neven, Tom, "'Don't Ask, Don't Tell' Must Stand," *First Thoughts* blog, First Things.com, December 1, 2010. www.firstthings.com/blogs/firstthoughts/2010/12/01/"don't-ask-don't-tell"-must-stand/.

Owens, Mackubin Thomas, "Repealing 'Don't Ask' Will Weaken the US Military," *Weekly Standard*, December 3, 2010. www.weeklystandard.com/blogs/repealing-dont-ask-will-weaken-us-military_520652.html?nopager = 1.

Perkins, Tony, "Ending 'Don't Ask, Don't Tell' Would Undermine Religious Liberty," CNN.com, June 1, 2010. http://religion.blogs.cnn.com/2010/06/01/my-take-ending-dont-ask-dont-tell-would-undermine-religious-liberty/.

Ranger, Mac, "The Peril of Repealing DADT—There Will Be Blood," *MacRanger Radio Show* blog, Macsmind.com, December 19, 2010. http://macsmind.com/wordpress/2010/12/19/the-peril-of-of-repealing-dadt-there-will-be-blood/.

Redman, Daniel, and Ilona Turner, "Don't Ask, Don't Tell—Anyone, Anywhere," *Nation*, November 16, 2010. www.thenation.com/article/156477/dont-ask-dont-tell—anyone-anywhere.

Suderow, Sasha, "Don't Ask Don't Tell: A Story Highlighting the Anguish Faced by Soldiers with Indispensable Skills," *Huffington Post*, March 12, 2010. www.huffingtonpost.com/sasha-suderow/dont-ask-dont-tell-a-stor_b_496565.html.

Websites

DADT Digital Archive (http://dadtarchive.org/). This website is a statistical treasure trove for information relating to Don't Ask, Don't Tell. It offers statistics related to DADT discharges and features links to polls on the matter. An excellent resource for reports and other academic works.

Don't Ask Don't Tell Don't Pursue (http://dont.stanford.edu/). Also known as the Don't Database, this site is a project of the Robert Crown Law Library at Stanford University Law School. The database contains primary materials on the US military's policy on sexual orientation, from World War I to the present, including legislation, regulations, policy hearing materials, testimony, and other valuable primary source documents.

Don't Ask, Don't Tell—US Army (www.army.mil/dadt/). This is the US Army's DADT page. It contains primary source information on the implementation of the DADT repeal and offers an interesting window into how the military is handling this historic policy change.

Knights Out (www.knightsout.org). Knights Out comprises West Point alumni, staff, and faculty who support the right of lesbian, gay, bisexual, and transgendered (LGBT) soldiers to openly serve in the military. The group's website offers information on and profiles of West Point graduates who had been asked to resign or forced out of the military because of their sexual orientation.

Lt. Dan Choi (www.ltdanchoi.com). This is the website of Dan Choi, an Arabic linguist and Iraq War veteran who was discharged from the military because of his sexual orientation. Choi has since become one of the most public faces and outspoken voices against policies that prohibit openly gay people from serving in the military. His website features his compelling story and links to resources on the topic.

Mission Compromised (http://missioncompromised.org/). This site is sponsored by the Family Research Council, a conservative organization that promotes traditional family and biblical values. It opposes letting openly gay soldiers serve in the military. The website features a succinct question-and-answer section that argues, point-by-point, against the repeal of DADT.

The Palm Center (www.palmcenter.org). The Palm Center is a research institute that conducts exhaustive research on the issue of gays in the military, finding that allowing gays to serve openly does not impair military readiness. The center's website contains numerous reports, articles, and other information about gays in the US and international militaries. Students will find abundant valuable information and statistics for reports.

Servicemembers United (www.servicemembers.org). This is the website of the nation's largest organization of LGBT troops and veterans. It contains resources for gay troops, their partners, families, and friends and up-to-date information concerning the repeal of DADT.

Index

A
Agape, 22
Alexander the Great, 23
Amos, James, 43
Anderson, Jed, 79
Anecdotes, 62
Arabic translators
  discharges of gay, 48, 50, 78–79, 81
  scarcity of, 47
Arana, Gabriel, 13
Aspin, Les, 16

B
Bandwagon technique, 63
Benjamin, Stephen, 45, 78, 81

C
Center for American Progress, 81
Chaplains, 54
Choi, Daniel, 78
Civil rights
  allowing gays to openly serve protects, 15
  military service is not, 25, 64–65, 66
Clinton, Bill, 7, 14, 16

D
Department of Defense, Perpitch v. (1990), 56
Department of Defense, US, 7, 17, 66
Don't Ask Don't Tell policy (DADT)
  has fostered anti-gay attitudes, 17–18
  number of discharges under, 8, 32, 77
  origin of, 7, 16–17
  restrictions under, 66
Don't Ask Don't Tell Repeal Act (2010), 9
Donnelly, Elaine, 73

E
Embser-Herbert, Melissa Sheridan, 15, 17–18
Essays
  parts of, 59–60
  pitfalls to avoid, 60
  use of quotations in, 84–85

F
Federal Bureau of Investigation (FBI), 40
Five-paragraph essays, 59–60
Fulton, Sue, 80

G
Gates of Fire (Pressfield), 22
Gay soldiers
  should not serve openly, 21–28, 39–44

should serve openly,
13–20, 29–38
will strengthen
military, 45–51

H
Harbin, Eric, 39
Hate crimes, 40
Homosexuality
changes in attitudes
on, 18–19
does not undermine
morale, 26, 44

K
Knight, Robert, 73
Koehl, Stuart, 21

L
Lieberman, Joe, 53
Loverde, Anthony, 79

M
Marshall, Robert G., 52
McCain, John, 15
McPeak, Merrill A., 25, 65
Military
countries allowing gays
to serve in, 54
dependence of, 41, 43
gay soldiers serving
openly strengthens,
45–51
gay soldiers serving
openly weakens,
52–57
use of, 28
Military Readiness
Enhancement Act, 50

Miller, Katherine, 80
Morality, 53–55
Mullen, Mike, 8–9

N
Ness, Christopher, 19
Nicholson, Alexander, 15

O
Obama, Barack, 15, 53, 55, *56*
on reasons for repeal
of DADT, 8, 9
Office of Personnel
Management, US, 15
Opinion polls. *See*
Surveys
Opinions, 62
Owens, Mackubin
Thomas, 9–10, 66

P
Palmer, Brian, 17
Paul, James, 15
Perkins, Tony, 20
*Perpitch v. Dept. of
Defense* (1990), 56
Phillips, Virginia, 9
Polls. *See* Surveys
Powell, Colin, 22, *23*
Pressfield, Stephen, 22

R
RAND Corporation, 16
Ranger, Mac, 40
Reagan, Ronald, 44
Redman, Daniel, 34
Reid, Harry, 53

INDEX 117

Ridicule/name-calling, 63
Rocha, Joseph, 13–14, *14*, *29*, *31*

S
Schindler, Allen R., Jr., 41
Stevens, John Paul, 56
Story, Joseph, 56
Suderow, Sasha, 47
Supporting paragraphs, 59–60
Surveys
　of soldiers on allowing gays to openly serve, *24*
　of soldiers on repeal of DADT, 53, 72–73
　of soldiers on serving with gay service members, 7–8, 66
　on allowing gays to openly serve, *16*, *81*
　on effectiveness of DADT, *42*
　on impact of allowing gays to openly serve, *48*
　on prevalence of harassment of gays in military, 18

T
Testimonials, 62
Theban Secret Band, 23
Thesis statement, 59
Toussaint, Michael, 33
Turner, Ilona, 34

V
Valdiva, Jennifer, 34–35
Virginia National Guard, 55

W
Winchell, Barry, 18

Picture Credits

AP Images/Evan Vucci, 56
AP Images/Hasan Jamali, 31
AP Images/John Chase, 23
AP Images/Lee Jin-man, 12, 27
AP Images/Susan Walsh, 36, 43
Gale/Cengage Learning, 16, 24, 32, 42, 48, 54
MCT/Landov, 49
Mike Blake/ReutersLandov, 46
Charles Ommanney/Getty Images, 14
Shawn Thew/EPA/Landov, 41
Alex Wong/Getty Images, 19

About the Editor

Lauri S. Friedman earned her bachelor's degree in religion and political science from Vassar College in Poughkeepsie, New York. Her studies there focused on political Islam. Friedman has worked as a nonfiction writer, a newspaper journalist, and a book editor for more than ten years. She has extensive experience in both academic and professional settings.

Friedman is the founder of LSF Editorial, a writing and editing company in San Diego. She has edited and authored numerous publications for Greenhaven Press on controversial social issues such as Islam, genetically modified food, women's rights, school shootings, gay marriage, and Iraq. Every book in the *Writing the Critical Essay* series has been under her direction or editorship, and she has personally written more than twenty titles in the series. She was instrumental in the creation of the series, and played a critical role in its conception and development.

8/25/15